CAPTIVE OF THE DEEP

LORDS OF THE ABYSS

MICHELLE M. PILLOW

MICHELLE M. PILLOW® - MICHELLEPILLOW.COM

Captive of the Deep (Lords of the Abyss) © copyright 2010 - 2018, Michelle M. Pillow

Third Printing July 2018

Second Electronic Printing November 2014, Revised Edition

First Electronic Printing December 2010

Published by The Raven Books LLC

ISBN 978-1-62501-207-4

ABOUT CAPTIVE OF THE DEEP
PARANORMAL UNDERWATER SHAPESHIFTER ROMANCE

Merman Rigel has searched for an end to his people's curse. Living in the lost city of Atlantes, women are rare and immortality has come with a high price-- loneliness. When a beautiful female is thrown into the ocean, her fate is in his hands, and this sexy mortal is more than this hard up warrior can resist.

Dragon Lords Series

Barbarian Prince

Perfect Prince

Dark Prince

Warrior Prince

His Highness The Duke

The Stubborn Lord

The Reluctant Lord

The Impatient Lord

The Dragon's Queen

Lords of the Var® Series

The Savage King

The Playful Prince
The Bound Prince
The Rogue Prince
The Pirate Prince

Captured by a Dragon-Shifter Series

Determined Prince
Rebellious Prince
Stranded with the Cajun
Hunted by the Dragon
Mischievous Prince
Headstrong Prince

Space Lords Series

His Frost Maiden
His Fire Maiden
His Metal Maiden
His Earth Maiden
His Woodland Maiden

Dynasty Lords Series
Seduction of the Phoenix
Temptation of the Butterfly

To learn more about the Qurilixen World series of books and to stay up to date on the latest book list visit www.MichellePillow.com

AUTHOR UPDATES

To stay informed about when a new book in the
series installments is released, sign up for updates:

michellepillow.com/author-updates

Thank you everyone who waited patiently (and not so patiently *wink*) for the final installment in the Lords of the Abyss trilogy, and for following me into this underwater world of mermen and their rescued ladies.

CHAPTER 1

LYRA HARNE HATED THE OCEAN. She hated the smell of fish, the taste of salt on her tongue, the briny smell in the air when the waves crashed against the wooden ship. She hated the creaking of the hull and the endless rocking, back and forth, back and forth, back and forth. Holding her hand over her mouth, she tried not to gag. It was a complete exercise in uselessness. Her stomach hit the railing as she puked over the side.

The fast clip of the wooden ship against the waves sent high splashes of water over the sides. Lyra was drenched, but she didn't dare move as she held tightly to the rail. Her heart pounded and for a moment it was only her, the rail and the long stretch of moonlit ocean, and the endless rocking back and forth, back and forth, back and...

"Just kill me now," she moaned to no one in particular, as she twisted the cap on her mouthwash. The taste of mint had become as familiar as the smell of salt, and just as hated. The few people milling around the deck were used to seeing her bent over in misery. She'd been that way for the last two months as they sailed from Spain to the Americas. The only reason she was on this ship was because her brothers and father needed her help. A very rich man paid big money for her family's sailing expertise. Her father, Captain Bill Harne, was the best of the best. It was said he could sail through a hurricane and come out smiling. Her oldest brother, Will, had been born for the ocean and probably spent more of his life on sea than land. The others—Jackson, Kristopher, Rocky and Winston—had varying levels of experience, but all of them were strong swimmers and dedicated to lives on the sea. Then there was Lyra, the baby of the family, spoiled by her mother and kept on land while her brothers braved the corners of the Earth. Her mom had been desperate to have something other than a sailor in the family. She'd ended up with Lyra, who wasn't really much of anything.

"Mom would have laughed to see you now,"

Jackson teased. "She would've said it served you right for agreeing to this trip."

"The seasickness or this hideous dress?" She glanced down at what could only be described as bar wench gone to sea. At least her brothers looked like respectable men from the 1500s. It was all part of the deal with the rich boss. He wanted the authentic Spanish Armanda experience. Apparently, the guy's great-great-great-something-or-other was an important part of Spain's history. The truth was, whenever the man spoke about it, Lyra's mind fuzzed out and she stopped paying attention.

"Now that you mention it, that gown does look a little less bulky." Jackson glanced at the skirt.

"I threw the petticoats overboard." Lyra grinned through her physical discomfort. "You try wearing a corset and fifty pounds worth of material on a rocking death trap. I still say that I should be able to dress like a lad. I'd give anything for a linen shirt and breeches at this point."

"Not up to me," Jackson said, slapping the pads on his arms. He wore an old fashioned linen ruff around his neck, an embroidered, padded epaulet, short stockings and puffed shorts much like those worn on the old Armada galleons. "This isn't how I would have spent my fortune." He eyed her with mock curiosity. "How is it you swam in from the same gene pool as the rest of us?"

"I'm pretty sure the family gene pool was dried up and I just kind of crawled in." She gave a wry laugh.

"You know, you could have said no to the trip."

"You all begged me to come. I'm the only one out of you sorry lot that can speak Spanish." She gave him a sheepish look, not feeling better, but definitely glad to have an empty stomach.

"I suppose it's better for you here than hanging by yourself at home. Mom wouldn't have wanted you to become a shut-in either."

"I'm not a shut-in. My job is online. I stay home and work." It had been three years since her mother's death and Lyra still missed her. Not wanting to talk about it, she said, "Tell me a story. Distract me."

"Did I ever tell you about the time we docked in Antwerp?" Jackson grinned. His devilish looks had been the ruination of many a young heart, but his heart had never been stolen. Hair as black as midnight and eyes that twinkled like stars—that was Jackson. And Kris. And Will. And Rocky. And Winston. Heck, even their father. Lyra took after her mom with dark blonde hair down to her waist and wide green eyes. Right now her hair was bound back at her nape to keep it out of her face.

"Yes," Lyra answered, "you did."

"East London Harbor in South Africa?"

"Yes."

"Robben Island on the Western Cape?"

"Yes."

"Hong Kong? Rotterdam? Pohang?"

"Yes, yes, and, oh please, not that one again yes." Lyra laughed, covering her ears, as her brother successfully distracted her from her seasickness. "Don't you have stories that aren't all about you and some lady you met at port?"

"Sure, but those aren't the good ones." Jackson motioned that she should follow him. "You empty? We should go. Captain needs you to translate."

"Man, I hope I don't have anything left," she muttered grabbing her stomach. "How long until this is over?"

"Less than a month," Jackson answered. "And about two hours less than the last time you ask—"

He never finished the sentence. The boat pitched to the side with a loud crack. Lyra screamed as her arms flailed in the air. She could see Jackson's expression fill with panic and concern as he reached for her. His hand missed her arm and she flew into the railing with a bruising thud. Her ribs throbbed in agony. Automatically, she grabbed at the first thing she could find, a long wooden post beneath the rail, and held on for dear life as the boat pitched in the other direction. Her legs tangled in the skirts as she slid over the deck.

The next seconds were the most horrific in her life. Men emerged from below deck only to be swept away as the ship was jarred again and again. She couldn't help them even though she tried to stop a few as they slipped past her legs, but could barely hold on herself. Jackson was swept away trying to reach her, captured by a rush of water over the deck. Lyra screamed again and again, begging and pleading, demanding that whatever it was stopped. But, in the end, it was no use.

"Monsters," a man yelled in broken English. "They come from below!"

CHAPTER 2

RIGEL THE WARRIOR ignored the tension in his gut as he swam slowly beneath the ocean's surface. His instinct told him they were close to their prey, and with each hunt's end there came a bittersweet result —they caught the scylla they sought. Yes, they needed to hunt the creatures. They couldn't let them roam free for they would terrorize the humans from the surface world, killing them by wrecking their vessels. But, to catch them meant the scylla would die despite the Merr's efforts to keep them alive.

Seeing the telltale flash of silvery black fins in the water beside him, Rigel narrowed his eyes and listened to the water. That was not the creature he hunted. It was one of his brothers.

'*Here,*' he said, directing his thoughts using their

mind link. All the Merr could communicate by telepathy in the water.

There were twelve Merr hunters in total, split up into four teams of three. He was part of a team known as the *Warriors*. The twins, Demon and Brutus, were his brothers. Rigel, though he was technically the youngest, was the leader of their hunting team—not that age mattered after a near eternity of living. It wasn't like their mortal days when age influenced rank or position. After hundreds of years they were pretty much the same and only clung to the memory of such things out of habit.

Aside from his team there were the *Hunters*—Iason, Caderyn and Solon. They were also in the water, nearby if Rigel's tingling senses were to be believed. The *Knights* led by Cain and the *Soldiers* led by Hrafn were taking a much needed break from hunting while the other two teams took up their duties.

As leader, he carried a vial around his neck filled with a liquid that would paralyze the scylla so they may catch it. The liquid was the only way to stop the creature. Unfortunately, if spilled, it could paralyze the Merr as well. Carrying it was a job that took much concentration and he would have final say when it came to capturing the scylla because it was he who needed to get into position.

Swishing his tail, Rigel navigated the dark waters to climb higher. His gills fluttered against his neck, filtering the water so he could breathe. Thin threads of moonlight danced above him, shining down into the oblivion below. He missed the moon, the stars, the sun and human land. Unfortunately, he couldn't break the surface to see the moon and had to content himself with seeing it bending and stretching with the current. One of the only things that could kill the Merr was surface air. It would burn the skin, but if breathed, it would destroy.

Brutus and Demon were two of the largest of the Merr race and identical in every aspect, from their long black hair to their matching dark eyes. Even their fins were the same silvery black color. It made them nearly invisible in the deep waters, even to their own kind sometimes. Rigel was a lighter version of the twins. His hair was dark, but not black, and his eyes were gray. When the sunlight shone through the waves his silver fins looked like ship metal floating in the water. It came in handy when having to swim undetected along the underside of a metal human boat. For this reason, they often volunteered for the more dangerous hunts.

Brutus approached, appearing out of the darkness into the dancing blue light. He motioned to the distance. *'I heard wood crack. The scylla attacks.'*

Within seconds the sound of drowning humans washed over them. Giant splashes accompanied the distorted screams. Rigel darted through the water, hoping this time they could make it in time to stop the creature and save some lives. Unfortunately for the humans, once the scylla started an attack, it usually ended it within seconds. It didn't stop Rigel and his brothers from trying though. No matter how often he heard such despair, it never became easier. He wished he could save them, but all any of them could do was push the humans toward the water's surface and wish them luck. When he saw the first piece of debris sinking into the depths, he knew it was too late for many of the mortals. There was no land for miles—too far for humans to swim. Perhaps they could float on broken parts of the ship, if luck was with them.

Though, honestly, perhaps pushing them to the surface and trying to save them was crueler than letting them drown. They were in the middle of the ocean, no sign of rescue vibrating in the water. Chances were their bodies would weaken and they would die a long, horrible death. If they managed to float on a raft, the hot sun and lack of drinking water would kill them. But, what else could he do? Wasn't a small chance better than none?

Rigel darted for a human, pushing him up toward the surface. From the corner of his vision he saw Demon was doing the same. Brutus swam on, searching for their prey.

'Rigel? Demon?' Solon's voice echoed in his head and he glanced around as he moved toward the next man. The hunter joined them, gliding his arms to hover in the water. The green-gold of his tail whipped back and forth. Like all Merr, Solon's tail and fins matched the color of his hazel eyes.

'Solon, what are you doing here? Have you come to help us?' Rigel asked.

'No, the Hunters seek another creature. It has been evading us.' The vial around Solon's neck drifted easily with his movements.

'We have the same problem, but it is close. I think we will have some luck this night.'

'You have been away from home a long time. You cannot stay out in the water much longer.' All knew they could only stay away from Ataran soil for two weeks before going mad. Once madness set in, they would never find their way back alone. Even going past a week was pushing it.

'Aye, but we cannot leave it. This is an old one. Very powerful. If we go home we might not catch it again. Who knows how many wrecks it has caused.'

'Then there are two old ones in the water this night,' Solon said. They both knew the danger they faced. The scylla were dangerous creatures. They were spirits of the water, mindless, reckless, forever searching. Two scylla together would be strong enough to push any one of them out of the water. *'I will get Caderyn and Iason. We will work together.'*

Rigel nodded in agreement. Not seeing anyone else he could save, he began sensing the water for one of the scylla. Brutus emerged to push a drowning human toward the surface. The mortal man was still alive and grabbed a floating piece of the ship's debris. Brutus swam quickly under his legs, making a current that would drift the survivor away from the shipwreck.

'The Hunters come to help us,' Rigel said.

Moments later he heard Caderyn call out to him. His dark brown hair drifted around his head, floating briefly before his stark purple eyes. The silver purple of his tail whipped once, pushing him up higher. Iason's green was soon flashing behind him, joined once more by Solon.

'You've been away from Ataran longer,' Iason said

to them. *'We will help you catch yours and then go for ours. You need to get home before you lose your way.'*

'He's a big one,' Brutus warned.

'Slipped by us twice already,' Demon added. *'Tore up this ship, though I see now that he had help. We were wondering why it went down so fast for as big as it was.'*

A cold rush of current, colder than usual, crept over them. They turned to the man Brutus had helped to save. The human's legs kicked violently, and they saw the shadowed form of a scylla gliding beneath him.

'By All the Gods!' Solon swore. *'It is huge.'*

Brutus gave a small nod, as if affirming he'd been telling the truth. All six Merr swarmed into action. Rigel tore the vial from his neck, ready to blow. The creature began to drift, nothing more than a dark spot in the water. It was a near shapeless, faceless shadowing. It made a dash past Brutus and Demon. The two brothers cut it off. Iason and Solon crowded its sides as Caderyn swam below. Rigel blew into the vial, breaking the bottom seal and coating their prey. The creature bucked, knocking the human up, tossing him high above the surface. The man screamed, but they ignored him. There was nothing they could do beyond what they were doing.

Both Brutus and Demon latched onto the scylla, fighting it as they dragged it deep into the ocean. The creature soon became subdued and the hunters were able to drag it more easily. Rigel let his brothers carry the weight, as he waved his thanks to Iason. He had no doubt they would have captured it, but with six of them it had been easier. For a moment, he thought about offering to help the other team. But, already he felt the dizzying pull of the water. He needed to get home before he lost his way. Hearing a splash as the human hit the water several feet from where he'd been launched, Rigel said, *'Go. Find the second. I'll push this mortal up and will follow my team.'*

'That way,' Iason said to his team as he swam away into the darkness.

'What is that noise?' Solon's voice grew faint inside Rigel's head as he grasped the drowning man's waist and pushed him up from the depths. The gentle feel of vibrations in the water alerted them to another boat. Rigel smiled as he let go of the man. Perhaps there was hope for the survivors this night.

CHAPTER 3

Lyra awoke in a sweat. Her heart pounded until she thought it might explode from her chest. For a moment, she couldn't remember where she was or what had happened, as she looked around at her surroundings in confusion. But, as the endless nightmares became reality, and understanding dawned, the fear turned to pain. Never in her life had she felt so much heartache. The stress of it built within her until she could barely breathe, or think. She wanted to run, but, more than that, she wanted to die.

"Just kill me now."

That is what she'd said as she stood on the deck, looking across the distant ocean. But, whatever force had been listening that night killed everyone she cared about instead—at least physically. For that same force had killed her in another, much crueler way. It killed her heart and soul.

"Next time I'll be more specific when asking things of fate," she mumbled.

Not for the first time, she imagined she was really dead and this was hell. Everyone and everything she loved was gone, presumably drowned beneath the waves. She was the only known survivor from her crew. Strangely, though, she was also beneath the waves. But, instead of a watery death, she suffered an eternal damnation. She'd been saved by a merman who suctioned his lips around hers and dragged her down into the midnight depths until all she could see was the glow illuminating from his eyes and all she could feel was the cold of the ocean and the tight press of his mouth as he breathed for her. Her limbs had been too numb to move and fight his hold, but her mind had been aware during each moment of the horrible trip. They emerged inside a cave filled with air. Only then did he release her. Tiny colorful lights had danced around her, and with that first deep, gasping breath, she had passed out.

For days after her rescue she had refused to talk, as if not saying anything would make the terrible delusion go away. And then, she didn't talk because the pain of her loss was too much to bear. She had been rescued and brought into the deep abyss, to a secret land beneath the waves. Some might call Atlantes a magical place, one that by all modern logic couldn't exist. Oh, but it did exist, and it was as real as the merman who'd saved her.

Mermen. Mermaid. The lost city of Atlantis. Or rather, *Atlantes*, as they called it. The Greek god Poseidon. A curse. An eternity. Apparently all real, and all adding to her living hell.

In truth, she had no idea how long she'd been trapped in Atlantes, or rather the palace in Atlas which was the capital city of the country called Ataran. Atlantes was the whole dome from base to top, the entirety of the floating underwater continent. Ataran was the country of land inside that dome. Atlas was the capital city. And apparently the locals loved "A" names. It was all she'd managed to learn about her new home—not from lack of anyone trying to teach her.

Days blended into what could have been weeks or months, or merely days. She couldn't remember. She was offered food. She was spoken to. She was led around the palace and shown things. Someone took her outside where there were trees and a dark blue watery sky pressed against a magical dome. She was introduced to people.

None of it registered, not really. They were merely passing moments in a blur of half-reality. And then, her mind woke up.

"We should go to the banquet hall tonight. The king has requested that we attend the celebration of a wedding."

It was the first sentence she'd really, fully heard. The low voice had been saying more, but she couldn't recall what had been said before that sentence. Though the voice was familiar in tone, she finally looked directly at the man who spoke for the first time. He was the one who had saved her. Rigel the Hunter. That's what the others called him. Rigel. She had heard that name a lot in her half-life fog.

His hair was dark, but not black, and his eyes were gray. No, they were more of a metallic silver. His expression was stiff, but she seemed to recall there being moments of tenderness around his eyes. She also recalled having hit and kicked him on several occasions when he had tried to wake her from a nightmare. By the look of his strong body, her fighting hadn't done much damage. Though he was dressed, she could still see most of his body from beneath the gracefully draping tunic. It only fell to his upper thigh. His legs, arms and one shoulder were bare. Her eyes focused briefly on his smooth, hairless chest, trying to remember what he felt like. Surely, she must have touched him, but yet her fingers couldn't recall the texture of the tanned flesh. Blinking slowly, she let her gaze fall to the leather strap sandals on his feet.

"We should go to the banquet hall tonight," Rigel repeated. "The king has requested that—"

Her eyes shot sharply to his face, cutting him off. He sighed heavily, as if torn between speaking and just turning and walking away from her. He had strong features to go with his chiseled body—high cheekbones, a strong jaw, eyes that seemed to pierce into her. Slowly, she nodded in understanding. He appeared almost relieved, excited even, by the small gesture.

"Here," he said, turning to grab a folded stack of clothing. "The tailors brought these for you. They finished them this morning. Since you had nothing to say about what you would like to wear, I took the liberty of choosing a few styles. Perhaps you will find something you like. I will be happy to order more for you. You can't be pleased with just the white gown Althea gave you to wear. Many women are particular about their clothing, at least here they are. I assume it is the same on the surface world. As I have said, I wish for you to be well cared for."

Had he said that before now? She couldn't recall. All her memories since coming to Atlantes were stuck in a mist, mere impressions that became fuzzier the closer she looked at them. He placed the clothing next to her on the couch and stepped back. She ran her hand over the deep blue of the gown, feeling it's softness against her fingers. Her lips parted to say thank you, but she couldn't form the words.

CHAPTER 4

Rigel sighed. For a moment, he thought his ward might actually speak, but Lyra stayed silent. Althea the Healer assured him that there wasn't anything wrong with her—at least not physically. So, it could only be assumed that she was choosing not to speak to anyone. He couldn't be sure if that was a blessing or not. The few times she did speak it was to yell at him—hateful, hurtful things, things that made no sense. Sometimes, she didn't even call him by the right name.

It was his duty to help her adjust. She was his responsibility and he was failing. Normally mortals who came down experienced a time of euphoria, where they could be told of their fate and learn to accept it before reality sank in. Not so with Lyra. She was unaffected by the euphoria. There was no calm acceptance in her, just a dull blankness tempered by moments of rage.

It had been weeks since that strange night when he brought her down. Strange because two scylla had been caught and three human women saved. The hunt was almost too successful. A blessing from the gods? Or too good a fortune to be trusted?

The banquet they went to was to celebrate one of the women getting married to her rescuer. One saved human, Lady Bridget the Scientist, had chosen the hunter Caderyn as her husband. It had been a long time since they'd had a marriage to celebrate and the entire Merr population was bustling with the news. The other saved human, Lady Cassandra did not fare so well. She had been taken to the countryside to heal, by her rescuer Iason, as the trip down had taken a hard toll on her body. Though, news did come that she was awake and doing better.

Then there was Lady Lyra. His ward.

Rigel felt his body tighten as he watched her hand stroke the blue material of his gift. Lyra allowed him to hold her a few times as she awoke from her dreams. The softness of her body pressed to his had been enough to drive him mad with desire. He held back, naturally, for when her mind cleared from sleep she often tried to punch him.

"I should leave you to dress," he said, hurrying toward the bathing room. His home was like many in the palace, a large square living area with low couches, an office, an adjoining room for sleep and a bathing room. Those in the palace took their meals together in the hall so there wasn't a need for much else. Lyra had been sleeping in his bed, so he'd been forced to use the couch. It wasn't the most comfortable of arrangements—not so much because of the cushions, but because having her so close only made his desires express themselves in vivid dreams.

Rigel pulled a cord hanging from the ceiling and stepped onto the showering platform. Water rained from the ceiling, sprinkling him with the warm drops. The fresh water wouldn't transform him like the salty sea water.

Quickly washing, he soon focused on his affliction. One hand fisted over his cock, gliding with the soap, as the other moved to cup his balls. After centuries beneath the waves without a lover to share his time with, he knew well the best way to please himself. Although sometimes the act felt more functional than fun, he had discovered a renewed interest in such things recently.

Rigel thought of long blonde hair and smooth feminine skin. He suppressed a groan as he tightened his hand over his arousal. Within moments he spilled his seed onto the platform only to watch as it was washed away.

LYRA HEARD a deep groan and turned in surprise to where Rigel had disappeared. The blue Romanesque tunic he had left for her to wear pinned over the arms to create gaping sleeves. She smoothed down the skirt as she went to investigate the sound.

"Are you all right?" she asked. The words were barely a whisper. She took a deep breath, clearing her throat. She became aware of her surroundings. The walls were flat, with an adobe texture. Beautiful designs were painted directly onto them. There was a small circular table in the corner with a pottery vase. Tiny symbols were carved around the base. Light came from above, shining through holes carved into the ceiling. She saw the glint of metal and guessed the place was lit by reflected light.

Another groan sounded, this one fainter than before. Lyra stiffened. There was something in the tone of Rigel's voice, low and arousing. She inched toward the door, slower than before. The sound of running water penetrated her brain and she vaguely remembered being led to a shower. Had he watched her bathe? His eyes on her naked flesh? She couldn't remember.

Without stopping to consider what she was doing, she touched the door and pushed gently. It opened by small degrees, just enough for her to peek inside. Water and light added texture to Rigel's naked body as he stood, head tossed back, hands wrapped around his cock. It was like a scene from a movie and she blinked several times as if the camera angle would change and she'd see something else. Instead, he stiffened, gasping as he came. A visible shiver worked over his body. Lyra took a hasty step back, hurrying to sit on the couch before he caught her watching him.

A knot formed in her stomach and she couldn't get the image of him out of her head. She'd been living around *him* for the last... however long it was? How could she not have noticed? He had the body of a Greek god and the man parts of a very human male. The realization that he was built like a human man aroused, even as it frightened her. If he was built like... And he could masturbate like... And he looked like... And she was...

"Fucking shit," she whispered.

"Excuse me?" he asked, sounding stunned. "Did you speak?"

Lyra stood and blurted, "I didn't hear you in the shower."

He glanced behind him. A linen cloth wrapped his waist, but droplets of water clung to his flesh. She took a step forward before catching herself. Time felt like it slowed into a series of small moments. A drop fell from his elbow onto the ground with a little splash. He blinked, his eyes lowering to the floor before lifting up to look at her through his lashes. Water slid down the side of his nose, curving onto his lips, only to travel across the seam. Her hand lifted. Her foot moved. She walked toward him. Mesmerized, she reached for his lips, following the moisture with the tip of her finger. He didn't move, barely breathed. His lips parted and her finger slid between them. When he didn't kiss the tip, she pulled her hand away.

What was she doing? Lyra balled her hand into a tight fist, forcing herself to remember the ocean. It wasn't hard. This man had been there with his friends. For all she knew, they'd wrecked the ship so they could kidnap humans, or drown them for sport, or to steal whatever was on board like underwater pirates. The thoughts successfully pushed her desire to a more manageable level. To Rigel, she stated, "I am ready for the banquet."

"The others will be pleased you are speaking," he said, hurrying past her to his room. She watched the door close before taking a long, deep breath. What had she been thinking? Had he responded at all to her, she might have let him kiss her, possibly more. Ok, definitely more. Tingling erupted over her flesh, as if her body had come to life for the first time in years. She wanted to kiss someone. She wanted to hit someone. Anger and passion overwhelmed her for a brief moment and she couldn't see straight.

Closing her eyes, she slowly managed to get herself under control. A low simmer of anger and grief remained, but it was easiest to feel and under- stand. She didn't hear Rigel until he was standing next to her.

"Ready?" he asked.

Lyra walked out of his home without answering.

"I see you're not talking again," he said under his breath. She paused, looking down the hall. Including the door she had walked out of the options were two other doors or an adjoining hallway. Assuming her direction more than knowing it, she walked to the hall and turned.

"THIS WAY," Rigel said, grabbing her elbow and directing her in the right direction. She jerked at his touch and he let go. He didn't try to guess at her moods for they made little sense to him.

Rigel's home was in the Warriors' section of the palace. There were only a dozen homes in total, split up into four halls, one for each team. Every hall had three rooms, so that each man lived next to his team members in separate apartments. They all owned a home in the countryside as well, for those times when they wished to get away from the city. Turning, he led Lyra away from the living quarters. They walked toward the banquet hall in silence.

The palace halls were clean and uncluttered. Large arches passed overhead as they walked out of the cave room and into the main palace hall. The city architects had glazed the palace bricks on the walls with a mixture made from the gemstones, which gave them a glowing blue cast. Light reflected from outside during the day, but in the evening torches were lit throughout the halls to give them a soft orange glow. The blue stone was accented with decorative yellow and white tiles to form beautiful, intricate patterns.

They came to a tall arched entryway. The banquet had already started and the palace's main hall was filled with people. Many of them were male and dressed like Rigel, though a few of the wives were in attendance as well, dressed in their best clothes—long Romanesque gowns and golden coils about their heads.

Lyra stopped walking, looking around the hall.

"They come for the banquet," he said, thinking she paused at the great number of people. He refused to tell her that many of the single men came to look at her in hopes that they would catch her eye. She was single after all and that made her a desirable commodity to the general unmarried population. The fact that she was beautiful only fueled the overall feeling of hope.

Lyra didn't make a move to enter.

He motioned to a long table set up at the front of the hall. "King Lucius wishes to greet you."

"Who?"

"King Lucius," he repeated, motioning to the king. She had met him on several occasions, but looked as if she did not recognize the name. "It is customary to greet the king upon entering the hall when you are new to the palace."

Caderyn began to approach with his rescued

Lady Bridget the Scientist. Rigel smiled. Perhaps the other human would be able to talk to Lyra and put her at ease. He nodded gratefully at the other hunter's attention. Lyra glanced briefly at Bridget before staring down at the floor.

"Rigel," Caderyn said in acknowledgement as they approached. "May I introduce my..." Caderyn glanced at Bridget, "Lady Bridget."

Rigel arched a brow at that. His Lady Bridget? Then, bowing politely, he said to Bridget, "My lady, welcome to Ataran. I was hoping to meet you. I would've come sooner but my team went back out to track."

Lyra snorted in disgust. Rigel glanced back at her. She didn't meet his eyes.

"Anything?" Caderyn asked.

"No, false alarm," Rigel answered. They had thought another scylla roamed near the top of the dome, but it had been a lost squid. Turning to Lyra, he hoped to draw her into the conversation. "This is Lady Lyra of the Explorer."

"The Explorer?" Bridget asked, studying Lyra. "Is that a ship?"

Lyra glanced up, but didn't answer.

"She's not talking at the moment," Rigel said to explain the awkward pause. He gave Lyra a hopeful look, one she didn't appear to see. "Lyra, Lady Bridget was also on the water that night with you, but on a different boat."

"Ah," Lyra said, her jaw hard. Her deep voice sounded bitter, as she said, "Then your people killed her family as well."

Rigel felt as if she had slapped him. Her voice dripped with disdain. Mortification mixed with surprise and anger. How dare she accuse him of such a thing? And in front of others? The full blow to his reputation would surely sink in later, once the shock passed. He felt others looking at them, their eyes narrowed, and he imagined the murmuring of voices spreading her words throughout the hall.

"I came and now I'm going," Lyra said, quickly turning to leave the way they had come.

Rigel sighed, not knowing what to say. He lifted his hand to the king, in an apologetic gesture. The king nodded from across the hall. To Caderyn, he said, "Excuse me. I should go with her."

Caderyn nodded in understanding and Rigel hurried away from the banquet.

CHAPTER 5

Lyra didn't know where she was going, or why she had said the things she had. She had no proof of their motives, only her suspicions. It was too big of a coincidence that the merpeople were under her boat at the same time it sank beneath the waves. But, she hadn't meant to say the words, they just came out, much like the rage she was feeling now. Tears burned her eyes and she wanted to yell, or hit something, or dent in the wall with her foot—something, anything, just to end the ache. She thought she heard footsteps behind her, but she didn't see anyone when she glanced over her shoulder. It didn't matter. She ran faster, trying to escape the confines of the palace. One of the halls had to lead outside the palace.

Seeing a bright light, she moved toward it,

knowing it had to be an escape. Soon she found herself outside. No one stopped her as she moved toward a long wall. It stretched around the side of the palace. Bright yellow lines ran along the glowing blue stones. Images of sea creatures were depicted along the walls, rising off the flat surface. Finding a narrow gate, she jiggled it until it opened and slipped beyond the palace wall.

The sky was dark blue, too dark for the daytime, yet it was light out. She vaguely remembered being told that the city beyond the palace was called Atlas and was considered sacred. From her place, she didn't see a city, but she heard the faint sounds of one. Inching toward the noise for a better view, she discovered the town nestled in a valley beyond the main palace gate.

From her vantage point, she saw the square grid of the roads closing around the circular center, and the even spacing of the buildings. The large circular clearing of the center was presumably the city square. The mermen took a lot of care in the planning. The city was just as she might expect an ancient city to be. There were no concrete sidewalks or streetlamps and the homes were squashed together forming whole city blocks with no alleys or inlets.

The roads were paved with large stones, and the homes had narrow slits in the wall for windows.

A man walked up a long path from the city toward the palace. She slowly backed away, intent on going the other direction. The city didn't extend up the valley and there might be an escape on the other side. Lyra didn't know where she would go, only that she had to go. She had never been one for large parties. When she was a child, she never dreamed of being a princess in a palace and she sure as hell wasn't going to hang around as a prisoner in one.

She kept her hand on the wall and her eyes on the city. Then her progress stopped as she hit a solid wall of flesh. Rigel. She felt it was him before she even turned to look. Lyra closed her eyes.

"I did not kill your family. I pushed those I could to the surface. I did what I could to save them, but it was too late. There were two scylla in the water and we—"

Lyra didn't want to hear him, so she turned to shut him up. Instead of a slap, she found herself grabbing him by his face and kissing him. His lips parted in surprise and she took advantage, thrusting her tongue beyond his teeth into the depths of his mouth. Instinct took over, in a way she would not have imagined possible before. The heat of his body drew her in and she jerked at his clothing, ripping the material as she tried to move it out of her way. Another rip echoed hers as he did the same, tearing at the dress he'd given her to free her breasts. Warm palms cupped her, pinching her tight nipples and releasing a wave of hot desire throughout her body.

Her pussy ached, so wet and sensitive. She pushed at her torn gown, until it slid off her body to leave her naked. Then, maneuvering his hand down between her thighs, she thrust his fingers along her sex. She moaned into his mouth. His tongue now sparred with hers, dancing and battling in the heat of the moment.

Rigel let her ride his hand as he broke free from the kiss. His eyes seemed to carry within them a great storm as he trailed his lips over her neck. He pushed her hard, smacking her back against the palace wall. The cool air hit her flesh, tickling the moisture left behind from his kisses. Lips wrapped a nipple and she gasped at the almost suctioning power of the embrace.

Her hips jerked. Her back arched against the hard tile until it was imprinted into her skin. His finger slid inside her, from what seemed like an accidental thrust of her hips, but once it was there, she kept him from pulling out by clamping her legs tightly. Rigel's gaze met hers in surprise, but she circled her hips boldly as she showed him what she wanted. The finger wiggled and she moaned enthusiastically. It didn't take him long to catch on as he thrust another finger inside her pussy and mimicked the thrusts of a cock.

Lyra gasped and moaned, riding his hand to completion. The climax felt good, mind-numbing and earth-shattering good. Her entire body shook with the force of it. Lyra hadn't been with a man for nearly a year, and then it had been about as casual and as unstirring as meeting a foreigner in a bar could be. But, this... This... Oh, this...

She shivered, her arms falling from his shoulders. She'd been so focused on herself, she hadn't noticed her hands digging into his flesh. Somehow she had managed to puncture his skin with her nails. Tiny lines formed in the shape of her fingertips.

"You enjoyed that?" he asked.

The way he said it reminded her of the confused look on his face as she encouraged his finger inside her pussy. "Oh, no, don't tell me you're a virgin."

He didn't readily answer.

"You've never had sex?" She gasped in surprise. Ok, so she didn't mean it to sound quite like *that*.

How on Earth, or would that be how in the sea, did a man as deliciously looking as him stay a virgin?

"I have," he paused, "done things."

"Things?" She arched a brow.

"We have pleasure nymphs. The dolls are supposed to be lifelike and I use mine quite often."

It took all her willpower not to laugh at that.

Rigel continued, "And before we became captives of the deep, there was a woman who I was very fond of. She did not make the dive down. Since the beginning of our curse, we do not generally pair up with each other for casual contact. Eternity is a long time to hold a grudge and if a couple has a bitter parting there would be—"

Lyra kissed him. How could she not? The poor, incredibly sexy man was trapped in the ocean with the body of a god, the cock of a porn star and apparently nothing but sex toys to use it on. When she pulled back, he acted as if he would speak. She pushed her finger to his lips.

"Don't worry about it, hon." She reached for his hard cock. Oh, but it felt nice, even though she had to negotiate the material that was hanging in shreds along his hips. Lyra jerked at the cloth, stripping him. "I know how to take care of this for you."

She dropped to her knees, grasped the base of his cock and opened her mouth wide.

RIGEL WATCHED Lyra as she took his cock between her lips and began to suck. The sensation of it was gloriously wicked and he groaned, torn between watching the erotic show and closing his eyes so he could feel every single second of the pleasure. Her head bobbed as she took him in and out, sucking and blowing, licking and teasing, teeth scraping, tongue soothing, hands gripping and stroking.

She went after him like a woman starved, aggressive and eager in her movements. Oh, but it was magnificent. Perfect, tight, wet magnificence.

Rigel gave her what she craved, unable to hold back even if he wanted to. His hips jerked and he exploded into her mouth, releasing all his pent up desires for her in a stream of fluid. She didn't flinch, didn't pull away as she swallowed him like a treat.

Then, licking her lips, she grinned as she stood. "Does your pleasure nymph do that?"

Almost weak, he shook his head in denial. "No."

"I thought not." Lyra picked her gown up off the

ground and looked around. He did the same. No one was out at this time of day, at least not normally. Besides, with the banquet indoors, almost everyone would be feasting and enjoying the company of the new bride and groom.

"Well? Did you enjoy it?"

He could tell by her expression that she already had her answer. Still, he nodded. "Very much."

"Why don't you show me this pleasure nymph? I want to see what else I can do that she can't."

Rigel wasn't sure what had happened to change her in such a way, but he would not question it for all the power of the abyss. He had begged the god Poseidon to bless and forgive him, to send him someone to ease the ache of loneliness. And here she was. She chose him. Out of her silence, she chose him. For only the will of the gods could have brought forth this transformation in her, just as it transformed his people. Surely this was a sign. She had come to care for him. She was choosing to be with him. His wife. His mate. His love.

CHAPTER 6

SEX SHE COULD HANDLE. Lyra knotted a couple of strips of material together to hold her dress closed over her breasts. Rigel had done a number on it. Then again, she'd done a number on him. Not knowing what came over her, only that she wanted to numb her brain. Rigel seemed the perfect project to do such a thing with.

She wasn't sure what made her get on her knees and suck him like that, let alone swallow the grand finale. But, for some reason, probably the same one that drove her to want to fuck him, she didn't care about anything but the pleasure to be gained from the moment. She didn't care if the surrounding tree line was filled with onlookers. Or if Rigel was a merman and she a human. He had a working cock. She had a pussy. That was all the logic she needed.

Oh, blessed numbness.

Before, all she could think about was running away. Now, she couldn't wait to get back to his home. She gripped her torn gown, not really caring that her hip was exposed or that anyone who passed would instantly know what had transpired. Public opinion didn't matter to her. Not now. Not with everything she'd...

No. She wouldn't think about that. Not that. She needed to forget. She needed Rigel to make her forget.

Rigel gently touched her arm, directing her to turn. As they passed by two guards standing before a very ordinary looking door, she adjusted her hands against her chest to press the gown tight. They eyed her curiously.

Both guards wore an Ionic *chiton* she had seen on other Merr people. The short, white shirt was a rectangular piece of material folded in half and sewn up the side. It pinned along the sleeves and fell just over the knees, leaving the calves bare. A single stranded belt cinched the material about the waist. The *chalmys* cloak draped over one shoulder in a broad sweep of green. It pinned on the shoulder with a circular gold brooch, engraved with a now familiar Merr symbol of the sun. Like most Merr, they wore strapped leather sandals on their feet.

"Lord Rigel," the darker guard said, nodding in approval.

"Vitus," Rigel acknowledged, a strain in his voice. To the tall blond, he said, "Brennus."

"Going to the banquet?" Brennus asked, unable to hide his interest in their attire.

"We have been," Rigel answered. The sound of his voice gave her a little shiver of excitement.

"We must be missing quite the feast," Brennus told Vitus. Both guards didn't even try to hide their amusement as Lyra quickened her pace. She still couldn't bring herself to care that she'd been caught in such an obviously compromising position.

When they were once again alone, Rigel said, "I apologize if they offended you, but they meant no harm. Vitus himself is married and Brennus hopes to one day become a hunter. The only way this can happen is if King Lucius appoints more teams or if a member from one of the existing teams does not come back to Ataran."

"I'm not offended," she quickly answered, not wanting to discuss his job. "And I don't want to talk about hunting or teams or going out into the abyss. In fact, I don't want to think about the ocean."

"I understand. I know that you have had a difficult time with—"

Lyra stopped walking, grabbed his face, briefly kissed him hard and said, "Shh. We're not talking about any of that. The only thing you're allowed to talk about is this pleasure nymph toy you have, any other toys you have, and the fastest route to see both."

Rigel instantly pointed the way they'd been heading. "That way."

She hid her smile. The promise of sex always shut men up. "Then this way it is. Lead the way and lead it fast."

Rigel obliged, almost jogging as he rushed through the hall. At least now she knew for sure that he wanted her—if there had been any doubts. She glanced back to the guards. They watched intently until she turned out of their view.

"The nymph is in my sleeping room," Rigel said the moment he opened the door to his home.

Lyra shut the door as he made his way to the bedroom. Her steps were more hesitant. Doubts tried to surface, but she forced all thoughts from her mind. Instead, she focused on the door, on the steps it took to get there. Inside, Rigel opened a small, slender wardrobe and stepped back so she could see.

"They are standard issue for hunters. They are the best pleasure instruments our inventors have to offer," he explained. Was it her imagination or was he a little embarrassed by the admission?

Inside was everything he needed to pleasure himself. The centerpiece was a synthetic woman, more lifelike than the blow up doll she'd been picturing. The toy's head was bald and her eyes closed. Designed to look like a woman, the nymph's body appeared soft and almost lifelike. Unable to help her curiosity, Lyra ran her hand down the toy's arm. Though more lifelike than any robot she'd ever seen, there was still a rubbery feel to its flesh.

"Does she have a name?" Lyra asked, biting the inside of her lip to keep from laughing.

"I call her, ah," Rigel paused before mumbling, "Venus."

"Venus. Goddess of love, right?" Lyra arched a brow. "I suppose that's very suitable."

Looking over the small storage pockets lining the inside of the wardrobe door, she pulled out a round, tan disc. The shape of it matched the receptacle on the nymph's neck. She pushed it in. Rigel didn't stop her. Instantly, blonde hair grew from the head. Next, she matched a second blue disc to the temple. The nymph's blue eyes opened. She pulled out the blue disc and the eyes closed. She replaced it with a green one. When they again opened, Venus had green eyes.

"This is amazing," Lyra said, moving to poke her finger into the toy's eyes. The nymph blinked, as if flinching. "Do they make male ones as well?"

Rigel made an uncomfortable noise. "There is no need to order you a male."

One blow job and the man was jealous of a possible plaything. Lyra wasn't sure if she was pleased or annoyed. "Merr women don't have options?"

"They protested most loudly when these synthetic women were first introduced into our society. But the vessels serve a great purpose. What else are men to do for an eternity with no women to fulfill our needs? If we Merr do not meet with release, tensions build and fights start. The unreleased sexual desire is called *the affliction*."

"And you said all hunters have them as standard issue? Is this because you're like," she frowned, not looking at him, "famous?"

"I am well known," he admitted. "After the excitement of a hunt, the tensions are always great. There is nothing like sexual release to bring the levels back to normal. If we don't, we become ill. It is part of our punishment from the gods—to be so sexually driven and not have a vessel in which to release."

"Again, I'm asking you. Merr women don't have options?"

"The number of women is limited. Most have married. Others have never requested such a thing."

Seeing what could only be called the on switch, Lyra couldn't help herself. She turned the unit on. Venus began to move her body against the door, thrusting her hips in small circles as her arms lifted and reached. The unit sighed, closing her eyes slowly and opening them with a dreamy bedroom look. Venus pursed her lips.

Lyra did the only thing she could. She laughed. Hard. How could she not? It was damned funny.

Rigel quickly shut the nymph off and it stopped moving. "There. You have seen it."

Instantly, she felt sorry for laughing at it. She could see she had offended him. He closed the wardrobe.

"Ah, don't be upset. I think Venus looks like a very sweet girl." What was wrong with her? She tried to say something nice and she ended up teasing him again.

He looked as if he didn't know what to say in return.

"I'm teasing you," she said softly, lifting on her toes. Lyra brushed her lips against his neck. Her hand loosened her torn gown and it slithered to the floor around her feet. She pulled at his waist, stripping him of his clothes. Once naked, she reached between them, feeling the length of his cock rise against the palm of her hand. His breath caught, an intimate sound that was somehow more intimate then she had been prepared for. "How about I show you just how sweet a girl I can be?"

Lyra bit at his neck, pulling the flesh lightly before letting go. His sigh turned into a moan. She nipped at him again, pressing her hand against his chest to walk him toward the bed. He fell back and she instantly crawled on top of him. Her flesh tingled everywhere they touched, as if he passed his energy into her. The sensation was strange, yet invigorating at the same time. She'd never felt attraction on such a potent level.

"I accept," he said.

She wondered at the way he'd said the words, but assumed he'd accepted her unspoken apology. Smiling, she nodded, focusing on the curves of his chest. He was in great shape, probably from all the swimming he did. She'd never been with a man who looked like this. Almost entranced, she settled against his stomach, straddling his waist as she ran her fingers along each and every valley of his chest and abdomen.

Rigel didn't stop her, didn't rush her. He closed his eyes, breathing deeply. Every once in a while, that breathing caught and he held it. His hips thrust in gentle movements beneath her as his legs worked against the mattress. The rocking pressed his hot flesh up into her sex. She slid against him with the cream of her body. The pressure hit her clit, simmering her already heated desires.

Rigel's hands slid up her sides to cup her breasts. He seemed hesitant as he tested the feel of her against his palms. She knew she felt nothing like Venus. Would he find her flesh strange after synthetic material? After a moment, he seemed pleased with what he'd discovered and began a more arduous journey over her form. He touched everywhere he could reach, sliding his hands along her spine each time she leaned over to place kisses on his chest.

Warmth spread from his hands wherever he touched her, working through her body until she felt as if he was inside her. Her flesh became sensitive.

Her nipples were hard peaks beneath his skimming fingers.

She wiggled her hips, sliding her sex along his stomach. The full length of his arousal bumped against her ass when she thrust back. Blessed silence filled her mind. Each moment was nothing but sensations—a sweep of the hand, a rub of the leg, a stir of buried desire. Pleasure trailed behind his fingertips, as he explored.

Time seemed to pause. It wasn't the first time she'd felt it when in his presence. Nothing else mattered, only this moment, only these sensations.

She parted her lips, unable to resist tasting him. Lyra had to kiss him, as if being driven by a force outside herself. She pressed her mouth to his, gently sweeping her tongue between his lips.

She wanted him too much and would not be denied. Eagerly, she lifted her hips, reaching down to bring his body to hers. The thick length pressed up. She hesitated, trembling before finally seating fully against him. His cock stretched her, but the pressure felt wonderful and she didn't mind the touch of pain it caused.

Rigel sighed, gripping her hips. His fingers dug into her flesh, holding her tight. When she tried to move, he kept her flush against him. His hips moved in tiny circles, keeping his body deep. Though small, the thrusts felt good. She moaned softly, wiggling against him, encouraging his deep rhythm.

Lyra pulled at his shoulder, rolling so he was on top of her. The position thrust him deeper still. He nipped at her neck and used his new leverage to massage a breast in his palm. His lovemaking became more aggressive. Rigel worked his hips, taking his cock in and out in a series of fluid motions. She spread her legs wide, digging her feet into the bed as she lifted to accept him.

Lyra grabbed his hand, moving it to her sex to show him how she liked her clit rubbed. He readily obeyed. The intensity was more than she could resist. Tremors erupted low in her stomach, shaking their way over her entire body. She stiffened, gasping as she came. He braced his hands next to her. Rigel groaned, his cry of release joining hers.

CHAPTER 7

Rigel held Lyra, watching her sleep against his chest. He was exhausted and yet he could not close his eyes. She wanted him. In his world, her actions meant she wanted him for more than a lover. Lovers spoke their intent aloud. Lyra spoke no such words. And, for a moment, he had convinced himself that they were mated and she was his, forever. Then, as the aftermath of their lovemaking took hold, his mind cleared and another thought occurred to him. Though he said he accepted her, perhaps she was not making an offer. The customs of the surface world were in large part a mystery.

Many were eager to hear from the new members of their society about the world above. Aidan, one of the rare males to be rescued decades before, was in charge of cataloging new artifacts and taking down data from new arrivals. With three women to interview, he was impatiently awaiting permission from their guardians. When he collected his information, he would publish his news to the whole of Ataran. Rigel studied Lyra, wondering if she would be willing to talk to the man.

As he drew his hand over her hip, his mind wandered. He thought of Venus and how the nymph's pleasures now paled in comparison to the real thing. The feel of Lyra's sex was nothing like the rolling sensation of the nymph. In fact, it was wetter, better.

He contemplated what Lyra's world must have been like, the things she lost, the people. Then, he thought of his own losses, of the brother who went to sea and never came back. They didn't talk about Nemus. They didn't talk about any of those who disappeared into the ocean. Some had left in the early days, trying to find a solution, tired of being tied to Ataran. Others were hunters who did not make it home on time and were condemned to be lost. His brother had been one who left willingly in those first years. Rigel had begged him to stay, to wait, but Nemus has always been a free spirit. Every time he hunted there was a part of Rigel that searched for his long lost brother, even if he didn't consciously think of it.

Lyra sighed in her sleep, adjusting her body. He lifted his hand, waiting for her to settle before touching her once more. The soft skin of her back and hip mesmerized him, capturing his attention as he stroked it. He could live in this moment for an eternity, and he knew from experience just how long an eternity could be. In his time, he learned that it was not wars or peace or politics that created life, it was these moments, these small things that were often overlooked—the brush of flesh, a sigh, a flutter of Lyra's lashes as her eyes began to open.

For a moment she looked at him with all the same sleepy wonder he felt and there was a connection. He imagined their heart beats joined and that he could feel her inside him. Could she feel him?

"I love you." He hadn't meant to say the words.

She blinked and the moment disappeared. Tears filled her eyes as she slowly shook her head in denial. "That is not possible. What you feel is gratitude, not love. When you learn the difference, you will see that lust is not love."

He didn't argue. She turned her back to him as she sat on the edge of the bed. The soft light caressed her, outlining her spine as she stretched. She looked thinner than when he'd rescued her.

"You haven't been eating," he said.

"I eat enough."

"I will call for food. It is my responsibility to see to you and I—"

Suddenly, she turned, moving to face him. "I am my own responsibility. Last night was fun and we'll probably do it again sometime, as long as you can promise me you won't lose perspective on what is between us. Sex is not love. Lust is not love. *This* is not love."

"I will call for food," Rigel repeated, sitting up. Whatever spell she'd been under was broken. "You may not be hungry, but I am."

CHAPTER 8

Sometime came much sooner than Lyra planned on.

There was something erotically fulfilling about watching Rigel's lips suck the tiny morsels of fruit, absently pulling them into his mouth as if he had no clue as to the seductive nature of the action. Each tiny orange pearl, about the size of her clit, rolled between his large fingers before being placed between his lips, bitten by his teeth and then sucked into his warm, inviting mouth.

It was too much. Her pussy ached and her clit throbbed in jealous protest. He sucked another one and she shivered.

"Are you enjoying that?" she asked, breathless.

He blinked in surprise, glancing up from where

he rolled a piece in his fingers. Clearly, he'd been deep in thought. "Would you like one?"

Lyra found herself nodding. He lifted the plate, handing it to her. She leaned over the couch to where he sat on the far end and, instead of going for the plate, she wrapped her lips around his fingers and sucked the tiny piece in. Sweet explosion erupted between her teeth as she bit. She nodded. "Mm, good. I can see why you like them."

Luckily, she'd merely slipped a dress over her naked body and her pussy was still free for exploration. She took a handful from the plate, well aware that she had his attention. Leaning back so her elbow was braced against the cushion, she tugged at her skirts and let one leg fall over the side of the couch. Her legs pointed at him and he watched with rapt attention as she took the tiny pearl and brought it to her pussy. She pulled the skirt with her arm, letting him see as she inserted a single piece just over her clit.

"Have another," she offered.

In his haste, he knocked the plate aside. Tiny pearl fruit scattered across the floor and the dinnerware crashed into pieces. She laughed. He didn't pause. His hands met her thighs, tugging her so he could angle his mouth just right.

With a groan that started before he even made contact, he drew his lips to suck the fruit into his mouth. Lyra gasped at the shock of pleasure. She grabbed another one from her hand as he pulled back to study her face. She again placed it next to her clit.

"Do it again," she commanded more than offered.

He did and again the brief pucker of his mouth teased her sex. When he pulled back, she had a pearl ready and instantly moved it into place.

"Again," she breathed hard, angling her hips up.

This time, he didn't pull back as far as before and she slipped yet another piece into place. Before she could command him, he sucked that one two. Lyra, unable to take the quick kisses, dropped all of them on her pussy. They rolled along her sex, some sticking to her moisture, others sliding down her thighs. He began kissing the ones that stuck to her pussy, sucking them gently as he ate.

After he finished, he looked up expectantly. Damn those eyes. They pierced into her.

Lyra parted her sex with her fingers, and exposed her clit. "Now eat *my* fruit."

The training worked because he moved his mouth against her clit in exactly the same way. When he pulled up, she pushed the back of his head, smothering his mouth tightly against her sex. His fingers gripped her so hard they would surely leave bruises, but she didn't care. Let him hold on to her thighs, pulling her pussy to his mouth. He moaned and sucked, concentrating on her clit.

"Lick my juice," she gasped. His wide tongue slid over her slit. "Ah, yes, like that. Lick it clean. Make sure you get all of it." At that, his tongue slithered inside her sex. She convulsed against him. He began to lighten his touch and she dug her hands into his hair. "Don't stop. Lick it. Get it all. Use your fingers to make sure."

A hand lifted from her thigh only to find her pussy. He thrust into her, wiggling around inside her as he sucked and licked. The rough texture of a wayward pearl rolled and pressed between her ass cheeks. His chin must have bumped it because his hand slid down to push it away. She thrust up, forcing the wet finger to slip next to the tight rosette of her ass. She bucked at the stimulus. He took it as more of an invitation than she intended and enthusiastically thrust a finger into her ass. The digit wiggled, moving like it had in her pussy. She felt him trying to force a second one in to join the first, but the tight squeeze prevented such a maneuver. His nose pushed up against her clit as his tongue fucked her pussy. It felt so good. She grabbed her neglected breasts and squeezed the nipples through the material.

Her climax came in hard waves. When he didn't stop lapping her, she was forced to push his head back. He gave her a meaningful look. "But you are still moist."

"Oh, trust me. That's a good thing. I'm supposed to get wet like that. You did very well."

Her heart hammered. His finger slipped from her ass and she closed her eyes, moaning in pleasure. She felt his weight shift and assumed he was getting up. Then, suddenly, she felt the thick tip of his cock along her thigh. She opened her eyes to see him coming over her. His face looked determined.

With a hard push, he thrust into her, filling her to completion. His hips moved with a frenzy, building the sensations once more. She gasped, crying out as it was almost too much pleasure. He jerked, coming inside her. Seconds later he collapsed against her, pinning her down with his body. The weight felt comforting and she didn't push him away. She would have been too weak to try anyway.

"I CANNOT GIVE YOU CHILDREN."

Lyra blinked in momentary confusion, looking across the bed to where her lover lay on his back. She hadn't asked about children. "All right."

"I thought maybe you would wonder about such a thing, being as we are," he glanced at the bed, not finishing.

"Bumpin' uglies?" she supplied, only to laugh as his anticipated confusion. It was strange how everyone spoke the same language—magically, she supposed for lack of any better explanation—but sarcasm and sayings caused confusion. "Getting our freak on? Doin' the horizontal hula?"

"No, I speak of us being lovers," he clarified.

Lyra laughed. "My mistake."

"I thought you should know about the children. Aidan tells me this is a concern that surface women have with their lovers." He closed his eyes and she took the opportunity to study his face.

"Were you in an accident? Or sick when you were a child?" she asked.

"In Ataran, the odds of you conceiving a child are poor," he answered, not opening his eyes. "Should you conceive, it's highly unlikely you will carry the child to its birth and even less likely that it will live beyond that point. It is part of our curse."

Lyra didn't know how to answer, but she did feel

disappointment. She had never thought of children, had always assumed that there would be time, some-day, with someone. And, if she didn't have children, her brothers would eventually. The family bloodline would continue. They would have giant Christmas celebrations and Thanksgivings, surrounded by the next generation. But that was before the shipwreck.

"I'm tired," she said, turning around to put her back to him. She closed her eyes tight, refusing to cry yet again.

CHAPTER 9

Lyra left Rigel asleep in his room. She didn't imagine that, after the day she had given him, he would be awake for many more hours. The palace was quiet in the late hour, the halls dim and cast with the stillness only a sleeping residence could give off. She wandered the halls, not seeing anyone as she absently examined the décor.

Not knowing where she was going and assuming that if she strayed too far someone would stop her and turn her around, she ventured down yet another passageway. The hall narrowed and curved, heading downward on an incline. She frowned in concern, but did not stop her progress. The bright colors of the palace faded into what could only be described as the gray melancholy of a medieval dungeon. This was not a part of the palace the king would want her seeing. So, to her thinking, it was all the more reason for her to go. What secrets were the Merr people hiding beneath their shiny surface?

A loud, screeching noise resounded from the distance. She jumped in alarm, pulling back against the wall as if it could hide her. She listened, waiting. The screech sounded again, but no one came to investigate the sound. Her heart beat at a fast pace, as she inched further downward. Fear gripped her limbs and fluttered in her stomach.

She came to a door and heard people scrambling inside. Metal scraped. The screeching grew louder, followed by a series of loud thuds.

"We're losing it!" a man yelled.

"Stop it. Don't let it loose," a frantic woman answered.

"It's not going to make it. The injection's not working," yet another male exclaimed. "There is nothing we can do but get out of his way until he's dead."

"We can't leave him," the woman protested. "Not like this."

"Don't let him touch. They're not Merr anymore," a third man said. "They didn't make the transformation into human form. We've done all we could. We should concentrate on a new formula for the others."

"They didn't sign up for this," the woman insisted. "We have to try."

"One more word and I'll have you removed from the project." Again, the first voice. The man in charge perhaps?

The screeching became more insistent. Lyra hazarded a peek into the narrow slit of a window to see what they were talking about. A nearly translucent creature thrashed against iron chains and bars. If not for the watery look of his skin, she would have guessed the creature was half merman, half human. Were they trying to turn it back into human? She'd heard people refer to the "curse" of being under the ocean. Were they experimenting on the poor guy? Did Rigel know about this? It wasn't like anyone stopped her from coming down into the prison. Surely he had to know. The whole palace probably knew.

Perhaps this was the real reason humans were brought down. They were test subjects for genetic experiments. The whole population clearly wanted to be out of the water and they were using humans to do it. Who else was down here? Her brothers? Her father? Or did they want more Merr to populate the underwater world? Rigel said they couldn't have children. Were they trying to turn humans into Merr and back again?

Almost desperate, she ran to the next door and peeked in. A translucent figure lay on a low bed, unmoving. He didn't look familiar. She hurried to the next one and the next, finding them both empty.

After her search revealed nothing more, she went back to the first door. The creature was convulsing on the floor while his captors watched in silence. It didn't take a genius to figure out the genetic experiment was dying.

Lyra couldn't let them know she'd seen what they were doing, and yet she couldn't pull away.

Shaking, she backed away from the door before running several paces back up to the beautiful section of the palace. She kept glancing over her shoulder as she rushed through the halls in search of something familiar.

CHAPTER 10

RIGEL AWOKE with a smile on his face. It remained intact while he crawled out of bed and slipped on clean clothes. Hope filled him. He knew what Lyra said about being his lover and nothing more, but he couldn't imagine that the pleasure they felt in each other's arms could be easily dismissed. Surely she would change her mind, would warm up to the idea of an eternity with him.

His optimism lasted while he searched his home, but as he looked for the third time into the shower to see if she was hiding in there, his hope turned to worry. She was nowhere to be found. His eyes turned to the door. He never locked it. Lyra wasn't a prisoner, yet she had never left his home without his escort before.

Though he knew he should not worry, he could not help it. Where had she gone? Why?

He thought of her outside the city walls. She had run there before. No one would stop her. What if she tried to go to the forest and the Olympians captured her? The surface wasn't the only danger the Merr faced. The Olympians, as they called themselves after the gods of Mt. Olympus, didn't want the humans brought to Ataran for they looked at the Merr curse as a blessing. They believed themselves to be goddesses below the waves, blessed with immortality and power. Before the caves leading into the abyss were sealed, when all were allowed to roam the ocean freely, the Olympians had been caught luring humans to their deaths for sick pleasure. It had been a rough time for the Merr people. Loyalties had been divided. Some to this day still blamed the Olympians for the Merr curse lasting so long without reprieve. There were those, who still believed that one day Poseidon would come down and forgive them, lifting them up into the sunlight once more. Rigel liked to believe the latter.

If not the forest, what if she headed north toward the mountains? There was no threat of Olympians in the mountains, but the terrain was rough. She could get lost or hurt.

Rigel didn't think, just acted. Once the fear took hold, he couldn't reason. If she was his wife, he'd be able to sense her in ways a lover couldn't. He would hear her thoughts and feel her presence. But she wasn't his wife and when he reached his senses out to her, nothing answered the call.

CHAPTER 11

Lyra pressed her back against the palace wall, listening as the sound of footsteps faded. The cool, hard tiles slid as she inched along. The hall looked familiar, but that was because it looked like the other halls she'd gone through. As silence resumed, she pushed away from the wall and continued on until she found herself at the doorway to a rectangular room. Long tables stretched over the length, dominating the floor. They were unattended.

Lyra couldn't resist. An eclectic collection of human artifacts were laid out in an orderly, yet cluttered, fashion. They spanned the ages, from anchors to hooks, to coins dating from antiquity. The barnacled pieces of a shipwreck were set on the floor in the corner, as if pushed away for later cataloging.

She walked around the table. There was an old pocket watch with a broken chain and clouded face next to the tarnished silver handle of a lady's brush. A hardened glove with delicate buttons wore a large ruby ring. There were pieces of yellowed silk, chipped vases, a Greek bust, rusted navigational tools, pewter silverware, pieces of a crystal chandelier, and sections of armor.

Growing up in a family of fishermen and sailors, she knew a lot about shipwrecks and lore of the sea. These looked like the recovered items of a shipwreck. On impulse, she reached to touch the watch. The once smooth surface felt grainy.

"Oh, hello, my lady," a man said. "I did not know to expect you this morning, or else I would have been here to greet you."

Lyra stiffened, quickly withdrawing her hand from the table.

The man was slighter than the other Merr in stature, with short brown hair and kind brown eyes. He wore loose wool pants and a shorter wool shirt. "I did not mean to startle you. Of course, I am pleased that you have come. I have been asking Rigel to allow you to visit. We have so many questions for you."

"Allow me to visit?" she repeated, unable to help her frown. "I need his permission?"

"They really aren't that good at explaining things, are they?" he said, more to himself. Then, as he came closer, he added, "I've been here for so long I have forgotten that you might not know everything we take for granted, though if truth be told, I've been relearning quite a bit with you new ladies in residence. When I said he allowed you to visit, it's not that he gives you permission, per se, more like he... permitted it?"

"Is that a question or a restatement of the fact that I'm a prisoner and you're trying to soften the blow?" Inside she hardened. Lyra thought of the poor transparent creature imprisoned in the palace dungeons. Was that her fate? They had referred to it being once Merr, but what did that mean, really? She needed to learn more.

"The fact that he is considered your guardian means he is in charge of you until you decide to marry. Lord Rigel will take care of you and it is up to him to approve those seeking your hand. Only then will they be allowed to court you. But, don't worry, you get used to some of the antiquated ways of thinking. He pulled you out of the water, so he is in charge of you. Kind of like that old belief, if you save someone's life, that life becomes your responsibility. And the person saved is in debt to the one who saved them."

Lyra arched a brow and said nothing.

He seemed to expect more of a reaction than she gave him so he added, "You can choose your own husband." Still she gave him nothing, so he joked, "They are pretty desperate for womenfolk. You can probably get them to do whatever you want."

"I don't suppose I could get one of them to carry me back up to the surface and leave me on a tropical island, could I?" Lyra wasn't sure who this man was. She tried to place him. It was clear he thought they knew each other. Unfortunately for him, she hadn't been paying too much attention during those first days of introductions.

The man's features saddened. "No, I'm sorry, didn't they tell you? You can never go back. We're too far below the ocean's surface and, well, even if you were to be taken back up to the surface, you can never breathe surface air again."

"So it's true. I'm trapped here." She slumped against the table, resting her hands against the hard wood to support her weight. Her head dropped down as she stared at the rusted frame of a pair of wire-rimmed glasses.

"Perhaps if I explain my story it will help you,"

he said. "As you well know, my name is Aidan Douglass. I was born in eighteen-ninety-three in a southern county of Scotland."

"Of course you were," she whispered, more to the table than to him. Her fingers worked against the wood, barely feeling the hard texture as the tips turned white.

"I was a scholar, a historian if you will, on my way to Africa to explore the great pyramids and to try my hand at digging up some buried treasure. Treasure hunting was all the rage. Our boat, *Bella Donna*, was attacked by mysterious forces from below, much the same way yours was. Since there were no women onboard when it sank, I was saved and brought here."

Lyra merely nodded her head and waited for him to go on.

"When I told Lady Bridget all of this, she suspected it might be time travel, but it is not. Time simply does not move here as it did for us on the surface world. Once your body acclimates to this place, you never get sick and you never age. I am over a hundred years old." He leaned over trying to catch her eyes. "If I do say so myself, the years have been very kind to me."

Lyra tried to chuckle politely, she really did, but the only noise she managed was a short sigh of air.

"You do not look too overwhelmed by this," Aidan ventured carefully. "In fact, you look mad."

"Please, go on," she said through tight lips. She didn't want to listen, but she felt she needed to hear it, finally hear it. This was her new reality and she wanted the facts.

"From what I gather, this society was the center of the ancient world. It ruled over much of the land—Greece, Italy, and Egypt, which was a vast empire at the time. Back then they were known as the Atlantes, which we know as the lost city that fell beneath the waves in one day called Atlantis. The people of Atlantes, known as to you as Atlantis, prospered with little effort."

"You're particular about the whole Atlantes-Atlantis thing, aren't you?" Lyra murmured.

"I like to be precise," Aidan agreed. "They were great warriors who were never defeated in battle. According to Merr legend, they were blessed by the god, Poseidon. If you're not familiar with him, he was the Greek god of the sea."

"I was raised in a family of sailors. I'm quite familiar with Poseidon," said Lyra.

"Marvelous! We must talk sailing later. I would hear of the updates made to navigational systems." Aidan nodded enthusiastically, his face animated with excitement. "As I was saying, Atlantes. Like all great civilizations, the people grew arrogant with power. In those times the afterlife was a grim place, not like the heaven I was taught about. With such a cheerless prospect after death, all these people could enjoy was their mortal lives. So they stopped worshiping Poseidon and began to worship themselves as gods on earth. They became lazy, taking all they'd been given for granted. There were no more battles to fight, so they raided their neighbors, taking more than they needed. One day, King Lucius, after much feasting and drinking, proclaimed to his people that he refused to ever die, for he never wished to leave their bountiful paradise upon the earth—land that was more beautiful than the kingdom of the gods."

"I'm sure that went over well," Lyra said.

"About what you would imagine when you anger a god. Poseidon cursed the city for its vanity and self-love. He gave them what they wanted. He granted their desire for immortality, and forever condemned them to walk on their earthly paradise and nowhere else. This land, he plunged into the water, trapping them so they could never set foot on mortal soil again. Here they have remained on the bottom of the ocean, their land drifting aimlessly with the currents. Now we are part of it, never able to leave."

"Your speech sounds memorized," Lyra said when he finished. She took a deep breath and then another. She stopped kneading her fingers against the table, but did not push up.

"That is because I have given it several times," he admitted sheepishly. "And I have had several years to practice it."

"I suppose you have to tell it to schoolchildren or something?"

"No. Children are very rare. I have heard of them, but I haven't seen a single one since I was brought down." He began fussing with his artifacts, inching them in one direction and then back again to align them perfectly on the table.

"You said I couldn't go to the surface? Why not?" Lyra pushed the glasses, following his example.

"Mortal air is one of the few things that can kill them."

"I'm not Merr," she reasoned. "So long as one of them shifts into fish form and does that lip suction thingy, I should be able to survive the climb. If we take it slow, my body should be able to adjust to the pressure changes just like a deep sea diver."

"I should have said the mortal air will kill us,"

Aidan clarified. "Once you're brought down, you can't go back up. Incidentally, you know they are mermen? You do not need further convincing that it is true?"

"It's kind of hard to miss when a fish saves your life by suctioning his mouth to yours like some sort of breathing apparatus. I was awake during the entire dive down. I had plenty of time to get used to the idea of merpeople. It was a long trip. Apparently, that's strange or something."

"Rare indeed. I have never heard of someone staying conscious for the entire trip. You must tell me about it in great detail. The others will want to hear your story."

"No," Lyra said firmly, thinking of her family. "I will never speak of it."

"But, the people will..." At her intense look, he let his words trail off and nodded in understanding. "I would like you to consider telling me about how the world has changed in the last hundred years. I heard the Americans did get their liquor back. That was a strange business, Prohibition. Though, trust the descendants of Puritans to come up with such nonsense. I've been going through my old journals since your arrival, trying to remember life as it was. Is it true that they found a way to make motion pictures talk? Bridget tried to tell me that ordinary people can even make their own motion pictures with little handheld devices and in full life-like color. But, I'm no fool. I don't believe that tale for a moment."

"You can believe in mermen and underwater cities cursed by gods, but you can't believe in hand-held camcorders?" This time Lyra did laugh.

"I don't know about these cam cords you're talking about, but there is unbelievable," he motioned around them, "and then there is just plain ridiculous."

Lyra picked up a coin. "At least it looks like you found your treasure."

"I never really thought of it that way," he said, smiling widely. "We've got coins from the Vikings, Phoenicians, Arabians and Spanish. Even one from Carthage. They seemed to have done a lot of scavenging during the Middle Ages. Before us, many of the humans brought here were from that time."

As he spoke, Aidan walked down to a table with broken relics. He lightly touched a leather bound book, one amongst many. Some were ship's logs, warped from water. There were a few novels. One in particular appeared to be a torn paperback romance novel from the 1970s.

He continued, "It's said that some of the Merr women used to lure the sailors into the water and carry them down, though I don't know how factual the accounts are as no one speaks of it. Though, it would explain how they got so many personal artifacts, like the coins and some of the jewelry. It also explains some of their speech patterns, like the 'my lords' and 'my ladies'. Most of what is here is scavenged from shipwrecks."

"I can see that."

"I can see what you're thinking and you mustn't. They are not responsible for sinking the ships—at least not since the Middle Ages and those were much different times. They merely collect from the wreckage along the ocean floor after there has been a wreck."

"So I've been collected?" Lyra frowned.

"That is not what I meant to say."

"But that is what you said. I was collected because I am female. My family is dead and I am not because I'm a woman? How am I supposed to react to that?" Lyra shook. She tried to hold back her anger, but it seeped out.

"You lost family?"

"I lost everything that night in the sea." She turned her full attention on him. "Since you seem to know so much about my situation, I want you to tell me who wrecked the ships."

"I..." he began to shake his head.

Lyra slammed her hand on the table, causing it to shake. Aidan jumped protectively for his artifacts, reaching his hands over them as if he could shield them all from her sudden show of rage.

"Who wrecked the ships? How is it the Merr know where to go and when? If they're not wrecking the ships, then they must know who is. I want answers. Who killed my family?" When Aidan's mouth opened but didn't release the answer she sought, she picked up the wire-rimmed glasses and held them up.. He gasped, reaching as if to snatch them as she pressed her thumbs into the center nose piece. It wouldn't take much to break the delicate metal.

"No, stop, please. It's not the Merr. It's the scylla. The Merr go out into the water to hunt and capture the scylla. They try to stop the wrecks, but they cannot always be successful. I have it on good authority that they try to save as many of the humans as they can." He gestured to the glasses motioning that she should set them down. She did, but she didn't let go of them. "There were two scylla in the water the night your ship went down. They caught both of them."

Lyra relaxed her hand, letting it drop to her side. Aidan visibly sighed in relief. "What happened to these scylla?"

"You don't have to worry about them. They never survive."

CHAPTER 12

"THE SCYLLA you brought back from the ocean is your brother."

Rigel stared at Gregor, unable to process the man's words for a long moment. Then, glancing behind the scientist, to where the scylla were kept in isolation, he asked, "Are you sure?"

"Yes. Nemus's transformation started this morning. It is him." Gregor waited patiently as Rigel processed the news. "We're sure. The profiles match."

Rigel took a deep breath. He'd been waiting, hoping, fearing this moment would come. Of course he wanted to find his brother, yet he feared what would happen next. With Nemus in the ocean, there was always a chance they would find a way to transform him back into what he once was. "Have you told Demon and Brutus?"

"I'm on my way now. There is a small window if you would like to see him. I don't have to warn you about what to expect. He has been out there a long time."

Rigel nodded. "And the other one?"

"Denhu. Our records show he left a few years before your brother. He began his transformation immediately and we lost him early this morning. There was nothing we could do for him. He was one of the fast ones." Gregor looked to the floor. "We don't know why the transformation happens faster for some than for others. There is no way of knowing how long they will last once we bring them from the ocean. The scientists are stabilizing him. I would give them an hour. After that, they will be expecting you whenever you are ready. There is no guarantee how long your brother will be lucid."

Rigel nodded. "I will be there soon. I have one thing I must attend to first."

Gregor left Rigel alone in the hall. Torn between going to see his long lost brother and finding Lyra, he wasn't sure which he should do. Then, as he took a step to search the halls one last time for Lyra, he suddenly stopped. If Nemus was the scylla they pulled from the ocean then...

"My brother is responsible for the death of Lyra's family," he whispered. A cold wave washed over his heart. If Lyra discovered the truth... If someone told her...

Rigel began walking with renewed purpose, desperate to find her. He had to get to her before someone said something. If she knew, he would lose any chance he had with her. But, how could he not tell her. It was her family. She had a right to know the truth.

Guilt, such as he had never felt before, filled him. What was he going to do?

CHAPTER 13

Lyra listened to Aidan's incessant flow of words as he walked about showing her his treasures. The artifacts were hardly mystical to her, not as they were to him. Though his assumptions about some of them were comical—like his inability to believe in the advanced technological impact of computers on surface society, while living in a mythical world using the advanced robotics of pleasure nymphs.

Lyra began counting his words in her head instead of listening to them. *Five...fifteen...fifty...two...*

"Lyra."

Lyra stiffened at the sound of Rigel's voice. There was a hard edge to his tone. Mimicking the sound, she said, "Rigel."

The show of attitude must have gotten his attention because he softened his words. "I have been searching for you."

"I've been showing her the artifacts," Aidan answered. "I had hoped to hear her recollections about the surface as soon as we were finished with the tour."

"That is fine," Rigel said. "I will come back for her later."

Lyra frowned at the commanding tone in his voice. He looked at her as if he would go to her, but then turned and left. Giving her full attention to Aidan, she said, "So, what is it you want to know?"

"Everything," he stated.

Lyra felt a tiny knot of dread in her stomach at the enthusiasm in that one word. Soon the emotion was well founded as the man continued.

"I think we should start with every exact detail you remember about geography. I have an old map drawn out that we can use. Then, perhaps advancements in science, medicine, politics, avionics, astronomy, geology, music, books—you must absolutely sing and recite every song and book you remember. You might think that you'll never forget, but after a hundred years down here the ditties don't come as readily as you might think. Oh, and we must have a full description of clothing, food, sanitation, industrial..."

RIGEL FELT his brothers towering behind him. For a long moment, only the steady, insistent drip of water on stone marked the passing of time. He knew they waited for him to step into the room first, but he wasn't sure he could. If he saw Nemus it would signify the end of their search. While their brother was lost in the sea, there was still hope.

"Perhaps they are wrong," Brutus said. Rigel glanced back. The black of his eyes gleamed with silver as the light hit them. He had pulled his long black hair back from his face, letting it lay against his back. His brooding expression matched Demon's.

"They are not." Demon sounded resigned. "The scientists would not make such a mistake. They would only come to us if they were sure." When his brothers didn't move, he pushed past them into the laboratory cell. His action prompted Rigel to move. As all three brothers came into the cell, they turned their attention to the floor. It had been a long time, centuries, since they had seen Nemus, but the memory they carried of him was still strong.

Rigel could no longer hear the sound of Nemus's voice in his head, or remember the exact look of his features beyond the representations they had of him on file. The transparent figure, curled into a ball at their feet, did not remind him of family. Yet, here was Nemus, their brother.

Rigel studied the scylla's face, seeing a familiar shape to his nose and angle of his chin. Translucent skin was as slippery as the ocean, damp from a near eternity in the water. The room smelled of the ocean, of the deep abyss salt and the muddy sand of the drifts. The blue of veins had already begun to show inside the watery shell. Soon, other organs would appear. Now they were just strange shifts of perception, like a jellyfish trapped in water beneath the clear flesh. When he stared into his brother's chest, he saw a fluttering movement where his heart would be.

"Nemus?" Brutus asked.

"Is he awake?" Demon frowned, leaning over to touch the scylla. His hand slid over Nemus's leg.

"I do not think so," Rigel answered. He too kneeled to feel the icy smooth skin. "He does not move."

"I do not like seeing the scylla like this. It reminds me of living ice," Brutus said.

"And soon he will melt," Demon added.

Rigel might not like the prognosis, but knew it to be the most likely of outcomes. "Nemus? Can you hear us? Do you remember Atlantes? Do you remember your family? I am Rigel, your brother. We are all your brothers. We have come to welcome you home."

Nemus convulsed, suddenly coming to life. He thrashed on the floor like a seafin out of water, bucking and sliding on the stone. A horrific yell escaped his mouth, the sound hoarse. Rigel and Demon jerked back.

Three scientists ran into the room. Gregor pulled at Demon's arm. "Let us tend to him. You can visit again later." He ushered the brothers out so they could try to help Nemus.

"I do not need to come back," Brutus stated. "That is not our brother. Not anymore. I have said my goodbyes to him centuries ago. Nothing of Nemus remains in that creature."

"Perhaps," Demon added, not openly agreeing or disagreeing with his twin.

"No matter what he's become, he is and will always be our brother," Rigel said. He thought of Lyra and her family, of what his brother had done to them. A pain gripped his heart and choked his throat, making it hard to breathe. Nemus was his brother and he loved him. But, he also loved Lyra. She might not want to hear it, but he loved her.

"Perhaps," Demon said after a long pause. "Perhaps."

CHAPTER 14

"I swear it's true," Lyra said, repeating the same sentence she'd been forced to utter after Aidan's show of amazement. "There is such a thing as an underwater assault rifle. It uses steel darts instead of bullets and the barrels are constructed differently. It is more powerful than that the underwater pistol, but the pistol is easier to maneuver."

Aidan grinned as he scribbled notes in his little parchment book. "What else? What else?"

"My knowledge of weapons is pretty limited," Lyra said, glancing down at the long list of items Aidan had laid out for her. "I suppose science is next. When oil spills, they have an oil-eating bacterium that they can use. The scientist, Chakrabarty, patented the micro-organism. I believe, and don't quote me on this, that this was the first patent granted for a live man-made organism."

"Live man-made organism," Aidan repeated softly as he wrote.

"Ok, I'm done for the day. My brain is about to explode," Lyra lied. In fact, she was tired of thinking of the surface world. Her brother Will had been the one to tell her about Chakrabarty. He'd worked to clean up an oil spill. Kristopher had worked on an oil tanker and teased his 'hippy brother', though in truth he had loved animals more than any one of them. Kris was the one who taught her how to dive and how to shoot an underwater assault rifle. She still wasn't sure how legal that outing had been.

"Lady Lyra?"

Lyra blinked at the quizzical voice. She hadn't been listening. Aidan motioned toward the door.

"I have come for you," Rigel said.

Her heart skipped a little when she looked at him, but she quickly hid the reaction. Saying a quick farewell to Aidan, she moved to follow Rigel. The early morning adventure started catching up on her and she yawned.

"Did you have a pleasant day with Aidan?" he asked.

"It was very informative. He had a lot to say about your people," she said.

"Oh?" Rigel stopped walking.

Lyra chuckled, teasing, "You should be scared."

"I have reason to fear what Aidan said?" He looked as if he would turn back to confront the man.

"No," Lyra grabbed his arm, laughing harder. He reluctantly let her pull him behind her. "I was making a joke. Never mind. I guess you have to be a surface person to get the humor."

"My fear amuses you?" He pulled away from her. "I do not need to be from the surface world to understand this."

"I—?" she began, confused.

"Go to our home. I must seek an audience with the king." Rigel turned abruptly away and left her to stare after him.

"It was just a saying," she whispered, stunned. Too tired to chase him down, and a little worried Aidan would find her alone in the hall and start quizzing her again on the surface world, she hurried back to Rigel's apartment. Between what she had seen and what she had learned, Lyra had lot to think about it.

"After Nemus is no more, I would like permission to take Lady Lyra to the north." Rigel stood before the king in his chambers, not pausing for the normal niceties of conversation.

"She still has not adjusted?" The king frowned, dropping the silken cloth he studied. He motioned to the seamstress to leave them alone.

"She," Rigel paused, thinking of how best to word his complaint. "She does not understand the Merr ways. It is my wish to train her before I unleash her on the populace."

"A very diplomatic answer, Rigel," the king said. He chuckled. "I might have to be careful, lest you come after my crown. I always thought you had the makings of a leader in you."

"I am honored, but I have no wish to be king."

"Are you sure? For some days I grow weary of the crown. When I took its weight, I never imagined I would be forced to carry it for all eternity. Or, if I did, I was foolish and young and did not understand the breadth of the decision." King Lucius gestured to the side in dismissal, as if such dreams were merely a waste of time and not worth considering, for they could never be.

"Birth decided your fate, not a mortal decision."

Rigel tapped his hand impatiently, thinking of Nemus, thinking of Lyra, thinking of his honor.

"So it did. And now fate has decided to give you a stubborn ward and a long lost brother." Nodding, the king added, "You have my permission. Take her north to the mountains. I do not like the reports I hear of her behavior in the palace. When she is not forcing her silence on us, she is screaming at you. I would not have her besmirching the honor of one of my greatest hunters. That is, I would assume, the real reason you wish to take her, so her words cannot be heard again resounding throughout the dining hall?"

Rigel stiffly nodded, remembering her comments about him killing her brother. Whether this is what she truly felt in her heart or not, it is what she said aloud. The fact that the king was also aware of this, stung his honor.

"You are an honorable man, Rigel. Her words will not change my opinion of you, but yes I think you should take her away."

Rigel nodded again and moved to go.

"Oh, and Rigel, I am truly sorry to hear of your brother. The ocean is a cruel mistress." The king didn't bother with false hope, or wishes to see Nemus well again, as he turned his attention once more to the project before him.

CHAPTER 15

"HELLO THERE, MR. SENSITIVE, FEELING BETTER?" Lyra glanced up when Rigel entered, expecting him to be alone. He wasn't. Behind Rigel stood two very tall, very brooding men. By the look of them they were twins, by the size of them they were formidable, by the expressions on their faces they were not amused by her words.

"Lyra," Rigel stated, his tone dark. "Do you remember my brothers? They were there when we pulled you from the ocean." He pointed his thumb over one shoulder without looking. "This is Demon." He pointed at the other. "And Brutus."

Lyra forced herself to stand from the low couch. "Forgive me, but no, I don't. Those first moments were a bit of a blur." Even as she said it, she got a flash of silver eyes in the water and a large black tail shining in a hint of light coming from inside the crystal caves where they entered Ataran.

Brutus arched a brow and she realized she'd been staring at his face. Without preamble he said, "There is no need to cast your eyes at me, my lady. I am not interested in a wife."

"I—" she gasped. Rigel stiffened. "But, I wasn't...I, ah..."

Suddenly Demon and Brutus began to laugh. Their expressions changed to instant boyish amusement. They both slapped Rigel on the back as they walked into his home. Without waiting to be asked, they went toward the kitchen to help themselves to food. There wasn't much, but that didn't stop their searching.

"Funny," Lyra mumbled sarcastically.

The twins laughed between themselves, talking in a half-language only they seemed to understand. Rigel sat beside Lyra on the couch.

"My words earlier were not meant to be insulting," Lyra said quietly. She felt her body pull toward him. All doubts and fears and anger seemed to melt out of her when he was near, erasing her unease and filling her with something else, something much deeper than she wanted acknowledge.

She couldn't look at him as she stared forward. She felt the presence of his brothers behind them. A hand brushed her thigh, a light gesture but one that held her complete attention. Nerves bundled in her stomach and she had the distinct recollection of being fifteen again about to be asked by an older boy to the prom. The nerves, the excitement, the girlish tingle, they all welled inside her and her breath caught in her throat, even as her heart hammered in her chest.

Lyra tried to think of all the things she should, the logical things that would stop this strangeness inside her body. Why did it hit her now? All of a sudden on such an ordinary day on Ataran—as ordinary as a day under the ocean in a cursed city could be. In a room filled with the laughter of Rigel's jesting brothers?

Rigel's finger slid over hers, breaking through the residual numbness left over from her dive down. She hadn't noticed it before, yet here she was, feeling his finger on her hand as if it was the first time. It caused her to ache all over—her breasts, her stomach, her thighs and sex. Only the laughter behind them stopped her from grabbing Rigel's face and kissing him like she wanted to.

Her mouth tingled. It was agony. His finger

stopped and she drew her eyes to his. He looked the same. Was it possible all the feelings assaulting her senses were hers alone?

She pulled her hand away under the pretense of looking behind them to the kitchen. It didn't matter. She could still feel his touch.

Seeing her eyes on them, the twins stopped talking and looked at her. It was hard to tell them apart except for their clothes. Brutus nodded in her direction and gave a meaningful glance to Demon, who in turn nodded once.

"You should bring her tonight," Demon said to Rigel.

"Bring me?" Lyra asked, looking at the man next to her. The fluttering again assaulted her heart. "Where?"

"To see—" Brutus began.

"I do not think that is a good idea," Rigel interrupted, standing.

"No?" Demon asked, arching a brow.

"It is a family matter," Rigel insisted.

"And is she not family?" Brutus challenged. "She is your ward, given the protection of our family name, and if I am not mistaken you will soon announce her as your wife."

"Wife?" It was Lyra's turn to stand.

"You were seen," Demon gave a short laugh, before saying, "out by the castle wall."

"Brennus and Vitus were none too quiet about your half-naked trip through the hall," Brutus added. "The king asks us often when you will make the announcement."

"We're to make an announcement tonight?" Lyra shivered. Why was the idea of being Rigel's wife not as repulsive as it should be?

"No," Rigel stated flatly. "There is to be no announcement. Lyra and I have an agreed upon arrangement between us."

This time the twins' expressions were not so cheerful. Brutus asked, "Then there is to be no wedding?"

"No," Rigel answered.

"And you agree to this?" Demon asked, shocked.

Lyra suspected if she were to claim she did not, both brothers would be forced to defend her honor against Rigel. Not wanting to see a brotherly brawl, she nodded her head. "Yes, I have agreed to it."

"Had I known that was an option I would have put my bid in," Demon muttered. "Aidan would have us think all surface dames want marriage."

"Dames?" Lyra repeated. "Yeah, that sounds like Aidan."

"Perhaps Cassandra will also be in search of a lover," Brutus said. "If Iason brings her back from the countryside we can ask her."

"Do not bother. There is no way she would pick you. I am the handsomer twin. Everyone knows that," Demon said.

"Is that what your pleasure nymph tells you?" Brutus teased.

Lyra closed her eyes and for a moment she could imagine it was her brothers talking, teasing each other. The ache came back. She took a deep breath, and opened her eyes. Softly, she said to Rigel, "I'm going to lie down and rest."

He studied her face and nodded. "We will go so we won't wake you."

After saying the customary things expected of her to his brothers, Lyra slowly walked into the bedroom and shut the door.

CHAPTER 16

RIGEL WONDERED what was wrong with Lyra. One moment she stared at him as if he had two heads, the next like she wanted to kiss him, a second later like he was the only man in the world, then as if she couldn't run from him fast enough. With all his centuries, he didn't seem to understand the first thing about women—or was it just Lyra?

"You should follow her," Brutus said.

Rigel glanced at his brother, unsure.

Demon nodded in agreement. "You should."

"Don't you have any food in here?" Brutus asked, turning back to the kitchen area. "No wonder your ward is so skinny. You don't feed her."

"All the wards are skinny this dive," Demon said.

"Whatever happened to women you could hold on to?"

"I can hold on to Lyra just fine," Rigel defended.

Both twins began to laugh, hard. Demon doubled over onto the counter, slapping it with the palm of his hand. "Too easy, too easy..."

"You are so easy to read, brother. Go to her. Make her our sister so that we may be released by the king to go back into the ocean." Brutus grabbed Demon by the arm and jerked him toward the front door. "You know we do not do well if we are land-locked for too long."

"To hunting," Demon said, lifting his fist in the air.

"To hunting," Brutus repeated, louder and with more force.

"Hunting," Rigel agreed, lifting his hand, though not quite as enthusiastically.

When the door shut behind them, Rigel sighed and looked at the bedroom door. He contemplated whether or not to go in. Then, thinking of Lyra on his bed, her soft body sprawled and inviting, he couldn't stop himself from going to her.

She rested on her stomach. Her head turned toward the opposite wall. He could detect her even breathing as soon as he walked into the room. Not wanting to wake her if she slept, he quietly stripped out of his clothes to get comfortable and slid onto the bed next to her. He ignored the fact that his body wanted her. Instead, he was content to hold her gently against his chest in the hopes that she would never make him let go.

Just as his eyes were about to close, she turned to face him. Steady eyes looked into his. Without saying a word, she lifted her mouth to kiss him. The caress was sweet, gentle, and it stirred a powerful yearning inside his chest. There was so much he wanted to say, to do. The secret he kept from her, of his brother Nemus and what had happened the night he rescued her in the water, felt like a lie. He was purposefully keeping it from her, so it might as well have been a falsehood.

Then there was his heart. Oh, how he wanted her! He wanted to love her, worship her, to be loved by her. He wanted these things so badly it made his chest ache and his bones weak. If only she would say it. If only she would be his wife. If only she would give him some hint as to how to win her.

Her tongue rolled against his, light and easy, as unhurried as her hands leisurely moving up and down his naked thigh. She made tiny movements, inching her hips closer. The tip of his arousal brushed her stomach, sending a shock of desire down the already hard shaft. Needing more, he cupped her ass and pulled her forward. The full press of her against his cock caused him to moan into her mouth. The intense pleasure filled him.

She smelled sweet and her lips tasted like berries. He licked along the seam of her mouth and was rewarded with a trembling sigh. He rocked his hips into her. The naked length of his arousal tangled in her clothes. Fingers ran up his spine, slithering like water trickling along the valleys of his muscles. His ass tensed as she made the trip back down. Lyra cupped a cheek, pulling him forward.

Her legs moved as she began to wiggle out of her clothes. When the bare flesh of her calf ran along his, he groaned. He couldn't resist. Rigel had to taste more, feel more, see more. The affliction surged within him. His lips moved over her neck, trailing kisses along the warmth of her skin.

Rigel maneuvered her onto her back, pinning her beneath him as he drew his legs between hers. A soft, round breast beckoned him from beneath the material. The texture of her nipple strained against the cloth dress. He brushed his mouth against it, flicking his tongue back and forth over the erect bud.

He couldn't stop himself. Her very nearness

pulled his energy from him. At first, he fought it, not wanting to open himself up like that, but soon he didn't care.

Her kiss became harder, as if desperate to taste him. She bit at his lips, not hurting but not too gentle either. Lyra moaned. Her legs worked restlessly against him, squeezing his thighs before parting in offering.

Rigel's erection bumped against her. Seconds later he found the slick opening of her desire. The memory of the wetness, the tight sheathe of her sex, called to the primal conqueror inside of him and he had to take her.

He reached down, finding her pussy wet and ready. His finger slipped into the tight folds, brushing up and down along her slit. She jolted as he passed her clit. He rubbed along her sex several times, pushing a finger inside her before quickly pulling back.

Rigel guided his cock to her opening, taking aim. His arousal slid against the tightening of her pussy, before he thrust, filling her completely. Her hand gripped his hips, urging him on. He braced his weight with one hand, reaching for a breast. He fondled it through the material blockade. Though he wanted flesh, there was something sexy about the way her clothes were tossed about her body. They pulled tight in some places and hung loose in others. She didn't seem to notice.

His world became a rush of sensations—her thighs against his, the wet slip of her sex, the softness of her breath, the heat of her skin, the pressure of her body. Her fingernails skimmed his back and ass, scratching his flesh. Sweet little noises escaped her throat.

He moved his hips, taking it slowly. Their lips met. He wasn't sure if it was his doing or hers. Lyra's hands pushed through his hair, holding him to her. Their tongues caressed, mimicking the thrust of their bodies. Tension built, but he held back not wanting it to end too soon. He waited to feel her tremble against him as she came.

Lyra gasped and let go of an erotically feminine cry. Her fingers dug into his shoulders as she tensed. Rigel's body answered hers. He came, jerking his hips as he released.

"Lyra," he whispered, unsure of what he was going to say.

"Don't," she answered. "Just close your eyes and sleep with me."

CHAPTER 17

LYRA WASN'T sure what caused her to slip out of Rigel's bed in the early morning hours and leave his home, but that is what she found herself doing. She couldn't get the image of the tortured man out of her dreams. Finding her way to the laboratory doors with some difficulty, she was relieved to find that the man was alone in the room.

She didn't know what possessed her, but she was suddenly pulling on the door in an effort to open it. What if it was her brother? Her father? It didn't look like them, but then the transparent body made it hard to detect features.

The frantic thought gave her hope. Somewhere, she knew that hope was pointless, but she clung to it.

She needed it. Lyra pulled harder. She wasn't sure how, but the door was suddenly open.

"Dad?" she whispered. "Will? Jack? Kris? Rocky? Winston?"

None of the words caused the being to stir.

"What did they do to you?" She knelt, touching the wet flesh of the man. She saw the shape of his arms and legs, noted the defined strength in his arms. He felt solid, slick and firm. "How can I help?"

The man stirred and she thought she heard him speak. "Ocean."

"Ocean," she repeated. Not knowing what else to do, she said, "Ok, I'll take you to the ocean."

The two guards would probably be at the opening of the Crystal Caves, but she could distract them easily enough. They would be eager for some kind of action, considering no one ever tried to break out of Ataran. If she told them Rigel needed them, they would run to his aid without questioning her. Then, she could help the man into the water.

"Ocean," he said again.

"I'm trying." She pulled at his arm to lift him. He wasn't much help as she braced her legs and hoisted him up against her back. Her legs shook, but she had a purpose and she wasn't about to stop. In this she was not helpless. She could help this man. She *had* to help him because she felt connected to him. She couldn't explain it.

"Hold on," she said under her breath, as she willed her feet to slowly move up the stairs. Sweat beaded on her body at the exertion. Her legs shook. The man's wet body soaked into her gown, making him harder to hold onto. "Hold on."

As she took a step, suddenly the burden lightened as water flooded over her entire body. The man dissipated with a giant splash. The sudden change tipped Lyra off-balance and she fell forward. Her hands hit the ground hard. For a moment, she stood, wet and shivering as she realized what had happened. The man was gone, spilled into a puddle on the floor, draining behind her down the hall. Seeing a hard block of ice on the floor, she automatically reached for it. His heart, maybe? The tips of her fingers touched the chilled rock.

Lyra's feet slipped again. She lost her balance and fell. Her arms flailed as she tried to stop her fall. The angle of her body was too awkward and she banged her head on the ground. For a moment, she was completely aware, but then it was as if a light was turned off and her mind faded into nothingness.

CHAPTER 18

ALL WAS INKY BLACK. And cold. So cold.

Lyra felt the brush of something by her arm, then her leg, but she couldn't see, couldn't feel beyond the currents that pulled her. The dark dreams were relentless, like the pressure of the ocean on her dive down. She could breathe, could open her eyes, but she couldn't see beyond the tiny specks of light dancing in the distance, couldn't move to fight the current pulling her this way and that.

Lyra gasped, jerking to awareness. She awoke feeling as if her body had been trampled by horses, drowned, and then run over by the bottom of a wooden ship. The hard surface beneath her back sent hot jabs of pain through her calves and lower back. Her temple throbbed and she moaned weakly. The sound caused her body to come to an abrupt halt. That's when she realized she'd been moving.

Blinking heavily through a bright light, she lifted a shaky hand and held it over her eyes. A figure moved, slowly coming into focus. Rigel.

He was dressed in a tunic. It fell to his upper thighs, showing his naked legs. His arms and one shoulder were also bare. Her heart quickened slightly, as her eyes roamed the strong muscles of his upper body. Despite the ache in her body, her sex drive kicked in. Her pussy throbbed with need as moisture gathered between her thighs. She was starved for him.

"We'll be at my country home soon," he said. "Do you think you can walk?"

Lyra tried to push up but her arms trembled and she fell back.

"Stay there." Rigel turned from her and lifted two curved handles over his shoulders. Her body shifted as he pulled the cart she was in forward. He began to jog, taking her over an uneven path. They moved up an incline. Sweat beaded on his back, adhering the material of his tunic to his flesh.

It took a moment, but she finally focused her attention past his body to the surrounding countryside. The peaks of mountains framed him completely. Above her, she noticed the top dome of the underwater city was much closer. She could see the outline of large fish as they swam by. It still wasn't close enough to touch, but the sight made her new life all the more real—as if she'd needed the reminder.

The path straightened and leveled and his pace slowed. Trees replaced the mountains, leading toward a sprawling stone house. Romanesque columns held up the roof over a long portico. She reached for the sides of the cart and pulled herself up. The lawn was trimmed and the house well maintained.

"Where are we?" she asked.

"This is my country home in the borderland," Rigel answered. "I thought it best to bring you here to..."

She frowned at his hesitation. "To?"

"To recover from your incident," he said.

"My incident?" And then she remembered. The transparent man had exploded into a puddle, sending her into the nightmarish world she'd been trapped in. She reached for her head, feeling for a hard knot where she'd bumped it. There wasn't one. "How long have I been out?"

"A week." Rigel again looked uncomfortable and

she knew he must want to ask her about what she'd been doing. He didn't and she didn't offer up any confessions. "Here. I will help you inside. I sent word ahead to have the rooms prepared. It has been awhile since I have been here, but the bedding should be fresh and there should be food left in the kitchen."

Rigel reached into the cart to lift her up. The sweat on his skin told of his long excursion carting her there. She wrapped her arms around his neck, as she looked toward the direction from which they'd come. There was no sign of the palace or the city, but instead a mountain valley. She knew she could have probably walked if she wanted to, but he'd already offered and her body was violently sore.

"Have I been ill?" she asked.

"Very," he answered. "Althea the Healer tended to you the best she could and we thought it best to let you sleep through the worst of it. Are you feeling better?"

"Better than what?" she mumbled. "Apparently I've been asleep."

He stopped walking.

"Yes," she answered louder than she needed to. With her head resting near his shoulder he could hear her just fine. "I feel better. Thank you."

Columns reached up both sides, supporting the

roof as it shaded the portico. Rigel fumbled to open the door. The house was unlocked and he carried her inside.

The front door led to a small entryway. Beyond that was a large atrium with marble walls and floors. Aside from a few benches, the atrium was barren. A hole was formed in the ceiling, letting fresh air into the house. Seeing a pool beneath the hole, she guessed it let in rainwater as well.

"You should be comfortable here," Rigel said. "You are free to go where you will."

He carried her past an indoor garden with stone paths and neglected, overgrown plants. Reaching a wide door, he walked her through it and brought her to a bed. Rigel set her on top of the covers. Instantly, her body sank into the comfortable bedding. She sighed in pleasure.

"I will get you food," he said as he left her.

Lyra nodded, even though he didn't see her. Stretching, she rolled on her side and closed her eyes.

RIGEL HEARD Lyra's soft breathing and knew she slept. Closing the bedroom door to leave her in peace, he walked back toward the kitchen to put down the tray of food he had made for her. Just as he was about to leave, he changed his mind and grabbed the plate and carried it outside with him.

Setting it down on the tall, cylinder offering stone, he said a quick prayer. It had been a long time since he'd done such a thing. At first when they'd been cast down, he prayed for the country to return to the surface. Then, he prayed for Nemus to come back whole. Now, he prayed that Lyra would return the love he felt for her. It was not lost on him that the first two prayers had gone mostly unanswered. Nemus was dead, though he did see him again. They were underwater, though he did get to see the surface from beneath the waves as a hunter. Though, come to think of it, Lyra did not seem to be warming to the idea of being with him for an eternity, though she allowed him in her bed. Perhaps he needed to be more specific in his requests to the gods. Or, perhaps it was time to stop the foolish dreams.

CHAPTER 19

LYRA'S STOMACH growled so loudly it awoke her from her sleep. She blinked as she pushed up from the comfortable bed to find Rigel sitting on the mattress next to her. He held a plate of food on his lap and a piece of fruit in his hand. At her attention, he gestured for her to take some food. Not needing to be asked twice, she reached for a large piece of fish and quickly pushed the morsel into her mouth.

Moaning softly as she ate, she closed her eyes. "I feel like I haven't eaten for a year." She was reaching for more before she'd even swallowed the first bite. Rigel placed the plate closer to her and watched her as she ate every bit of it.

When she'd finished, he said, "I was worried

about you. Althea assured me you would heal, but I was concerned when you did not wake up."

"Is that man dead?" she asked.

"It was not a man. He was called a scylla." Rigel frowned. "You should not have taken him from his cell."

"I couldn't have left him there. He was dying." Lyra stretched her arms over her head, still a little sleepy despite her overlong nap.

"The king was not pleased with your interference. We work hard to ensure the scylla are pulled from the ocean. If you would have succeeded in your foolish mission, we might have spent the next hundred years trying to track him again."

"I'm not worried about the king," she said absently. "Men don't scare me. I can talk myself out of the trouble easily enough."

"He is very angry at the stunt."

"The king will get over it," Lyra said, not sure what was making her so confident of the fact. "Especially when I tell him about the spell I was under. The second I touched that creature, I felt him. I felt bad for him. I felt his emptiness. He was lost and scared and I was trying to help him. He wanted to go to the ocean and his desire to be free filled me."

"But—"

"And you will protect me," she said, smiling. Lyra decided it was best not to tell him what she thought before going to rescue the scylla from his prison. He didn't need to know about her unfounded suspicions or her half-baked mental accusations. "You have to. I'm your ward."

"Yes, but he is the king."

Lyra smiled at that, letting her lashes drop. "Are you saying you would choose him over me?" She let her hand slide forward onto his chest. Suddenly, she didn't feel so tired. She liked the way his breath caught and his heart quickened. He always responded to her and the fact made her want him more. Her lips parted as she leaned closer to his face. "Who would you choose?"

"I would choose you," he said without hesitation, leaning forward to close the distance between their mouths. His kiss was deep and instantly passionate. His tongue slipped along the seam of her lips, parting them. She opened naturally to him, not even thinking to resist. His familiar taste urged her body to inch closer.

Rigel's hands massaged their way up her back in small circles. She moaned at the relaxing pleasure of his touch.

"Then I accept," she breathed, not looking at him.

"Accept?" He paused in his kiss.

"Take me," she said. Being with him felt right.

Soon hands found flesh, peeling back all obstacles as they came together. He captured her nipple, suctioning his mouth to her breast. His tongue twirled around the erect tip in small, agonizing circles. Lyra moaned. She ran her hands into his hair as her body worked restlessly against him. Her fingernails scraped lightly at his scalp before moving down to his shoulder.

His mouth traveled down her body, sprinkling light kisses over her flesh. He maneuvered his body over hers, sliding between her parting legs. Rigel braced her thighs with his hands, holding them open. Slowly he drew his mouth to her sex, teasing it with his breath and brushing kisses.

She thrust her hips up, urging him to hurry. He didn't hurry, instead taking his time. His hands moved around to cup her ass. Lyra jerked, moaning softly at the pleasure. After what seemed like an eternity, his mouth closed over her sex. She cried out as his tongue twirled over her clit. His fingers ventured along the soft folds of her pussy, parting them as they thrust inside.

"Come here," she demanded, pulling up on his arms.

He braced his weight on his hands, pressing his body along hers. His heat warmed her, filling her with tingling promise. The taste of her desire was on his lips as he kissed her once more. The full extent of his passion skimmed her thigh as he drew his hips forward. She met him eagerly. The first press of hot flesh penetrating her body caused her to stiffen in anticipation.

"Yes," she moaned. "Yes, yes..."

He thrust, his body filling her, stretching her. They were instantly caught up in a frenzied rhythm. Every second became a sensation, a pleasure. Every brush of flesh became an eternity within a moment. When she came, Lyra cried out, the sound of her voice mingling with his. This was what she wanted. He was what she wanted.

This was perfection.

CHAPTER 20

EVERY TIME she closed her eyes the coldness was waiting for her. It consumed her, called to her, made her want to drift and be a part of it even as her soul ached to go home. She tried to fight it, but the current was too strong, too endless. There was no end to it, no hope, no one to talk to. She sensed life beyond the darkness, but it stayed just beyond her reach. And then there was a tinge of hope. She felt vibrations in the darkness, a sign of life coming from above. She reached for it, moved for it, tried to grab onto it.

Her body crashed into a hard surface, but instead of grabbing hold it slid past her. She aimed for it again, and again she crashed and slipped. The vibrations grew stronger, spreading out around her. She reached for it again and again and again, but it was hopeless. The more she tried to connect, the more impossible it became until the vibrations stopped and she was left feeling worse than before.

Lyra gasped, pushing up on the bed. The remnants of sleep haunted her and for a moment she didn't know where she was. A warm hand caressed her thigh and instantly the coldness left her.

"You kick in your sleep," Rigel said.

She was glad he was there. Without thought, she snuggled into his warmth. "I keep dreaming that I'm trapped in darkness. Like when we dived down, only I'm alone and at the whim of the currents until I feel a vibration." She gave a small yawn. "I kept hitting my body into something hard, trying to grab hold, but I couldn't seem to get it."

"Nemus," he whispered.

"What?" she asked, not understanding.

"I have heard that when the scylla die, they can imprint part of their memories onto the person they touch. It is why they are locked in a cell for those final moments. The burden of their restless spirit is hard to live with." Rigel's hand tightened on her leg. "I am sorry, but I think you have been imprinted with the scylla's memories."

"Scylla?" Lyra pushed up. "That creature was a...? He asked me to take him to the ocean. If I managed to get him into the water." She covered her mouth in horror. "That thing killed my family?"

"There are many scylla, but yes, that was the one who killed your family." Rigel's fingers brushed over her as he reached for her, but she moved out of his grasp.

"You called him Nemus." Lyra reached to feel for Rigel's face in the darkness. "You know him by name?"

"Knew." Rigel stiffened beneath her fingers. "I knew him long ago, before he was lost in the ocean, when he was like me, a Merr. He left our world in search of a better existence. Instead, he found the nothingness of the ocean."

"That is why you feel obligated to hunt them. They're your own people." Lyra pushed up from the bed, succeeding in putting more space between them as she tried to comprehend what had happened. Her legs wobbled as her feet touched the floor. "I feel him inside my head." She grabbed her hair, pulling it away from her scalp as if doing so would end the torment of the cold, watery existence in her dreams. "He was so lonely and lost. He just wanted to find something to hold on to, but he couldn't. He kept reaching for the ship, trying to grab hold of it, but every time he crashed into it his body would fall apart and he'd have to try again. He didn't know what he was doing. I understand that, but then I see my family. I see those people sliding off the ship..." She couldn't continue as her voice cracked.

Lyra breathed heavily. She wanted to hate the creature, but she understood it too well. It was nothing more than a force of nature. Her family wasn't murdered. They were victims of a natural disaster. Knowing didn't make it easier to deal with the loss, but it did take away her hatred for the creatures of the ocean.

"There is more I should tell you," Rigel said. She heard the hesitance in him. When she turned to the sound of his voice, she saw a soft glow where his eyes were. It was the same glow that had guided them in the water on the dive down. "Nemus was my brother. I've been looking for him for centuries. It was my brother who wrecked your ship."

Lyra took a deep breath. Then another. And then another. Finally, after careful thought, she said, "Then you have lost someone to the ocean as well. I am sorry you lost a brother, Rigel. I suppose we both understand what each other is feeling, huh? It's not easy to lose family."

The bed shifted as he moved. "You do not sound as if you hate me."

"Hate you?" she repeated in surprise. "Rigel, how could you think I hated you?"

"You blame my people for your family."

"I blamed everyone and everything for my family—you, your people, my god, your gods, the ocean, nature, the scylla, myself, my family for being sailors, my mother for not insisting they all stay landlocked. None of the blame was fair. I was just so lost and hurt. Please, understand, I'm trying. I miss them so much. Sometimes, it's like they're not even dead. It's like they've gone to sea and I can imagine that they're out there, safe on some boat."

"Perhaps they are. We pushed many of the people toward the surface and tried to direct the current toward land. Perhaps they were saved."

"Perhaps," she repeated, liking the idea. In truth, she had no proof they weren't saved. "Two boats did go down that night. Someone would have to notice that neither boat checked in. The guy who commissioned us had a lot of money. Surely his company sent someone out to investigate. They have satellite tracking and the other ship was a science vessel." She glanced upward, thinking of the surface world. "Yes, perhaps."

"I promise you, if there is a way to learn the

truth, I will do it." Rigel didn't sound convinced that he ever would, but she knew he would try.

"Rigel. Aidan was saying something about my becoming Merr once I acclimated to the underwater. Does that mean I'll be able to swim in the ocean? I mean, will I swim like you? Like a mermaid?"

She saw the glow of his eyes nod in affirmation.

"Then I think I know of a way I can contact them. When we were little, we would play a game where we'd send out messages in a bottle and see if they'd get an answer. Sometimes, they'd come back. If I can get to the coastline where we used to play then maybe I could get a message to my brothers. If they're alive, they will find it. And, maybe, they can get a message to me. I can tell them to hide the letter in the ocean where we can find it."

"Lyra, wait, to become Merr you must first drown. I am told it is painful and—"

"Will you be down there with me?"

"Yes," he said.

"And you won't leave me alone?" she insisted.

"Never," he said.

"Then I will do it. As soon as we get back to the palace, I will—"

"But we just got here," he protested. Rigel moved toward her. She leaned forward so he could find her more easily in the dark. His hand touched her hip and she shivered.

Oh, I love your touch, she thought.

"And I love touching you," he answered.

She smiled before stiffening. "What are you talking about? I didn't say that out loud."

"Didn't you?"

"No, I thought it." She frowned. *Just like I'm thinking this now...I really miss hot dogs.*

"What is a hot dog?"

She gasped. "How long have you been in my head? I mean, oh..." Suddenly, she thought of all the wickedly delightful things she'd imagined about him during their time together. Then she tried not to think of all those wickedly delightful things, but in doing so, she thought of more.

"I love you, too, Lyra. And yes, I would be honored to be joined with you as your husband."

"I didn't think that!" she said in protest. Though the words gave her pleasure, she couldn't understand what was happening.

The fact I can hear you, and you me, is proof enough that it is what you want. We are joined, Lyra. You are mine and I am yours.

"Did you think that or say that?" She asked, confused. Then, shaking her head, she added, "No, don't answer. Don't think of anything. Don't say anything. Just sit there."

The image of her own naked body flashed through her and she felt a strong stirring of desire. She couldn't tell if it was his or hers. The force of it caused her to let loose a light sigh of pleasure and need. Instantly, she pushed onto the bed, searching for him. He was already naked and she took full advantage. Her hands moved along his flesh. She loved the feel of him, the smell, the heat, the tingling sensations that erupted wherever they touched. His hands were at a disadvantage as they met with her clothing. He tugged at it impatiently, ripping the delicate material in his haste to part her from it.

He rolled her onto her back, pinning her with his weight. His hands massaged her breasts, peaking the nipples as he worked his way downward. Her legs parted naturally so he could slip between them. Already she was wet, ready for his claiming. Rigel's thoughts entered her in a series of random sensations —soft breasts, sweet smell, hard cock ready to be sheathed.

"I do love you," she whispered, as his cock found the entrance along her sex. "I do want to be with you. Forever, Rigel."

"I know." He thrust forward, filling her

completely. She moaned, closing her eyes tightly. "For you have no other choice. If you'd said otherwise, I would simply spend forever convincing you."

Before she could answer, he pulled back and thrust again. Their bodies became a frenzy of movement. She gripped his shoulders. His hands pinned her into place as he pressed into the mattress at her sides. His lips molded to hers, kissing her deeply. Hips propelled forward, taking her hard and deep and fast. Their bodies bounced. Her breasts bobbed, the nipples brushing to his chest. He took her leg, hooking it with his elbow to lift it onto his shoulder. He must have heard the thought because it was exactly the position she wanted.

The pleasure was too intense to resist. Tremors erupted like a geyser, spurting over her in hot waves as he came into her body. Their climax joined, intensified by their connection. She was still trembling when he finished. He slid his cock from her and rolled to the side in blissful exhaustion.

"Wow," she whispered. "That was...wow."

"Give me a moment. As soon as I recover I will wow you again." He touched her thigh close to her sex. His finger lifted to trace a light line over her pussy. Her hips jerked in response and he chuckled.

"Perhaps we can wait a few days before going

back to the palace," she said. "There is no need to rush out of bed so fast."

"A few days?"

"Perhaps more. We'll see how long you can last, hunter." She reached for his semi-erect cock and began to rub it as he rubbed her. Then, pushing up, she moved to straddle his waist while facing his feet. She slid her pussy along his chest until she was leaning over his cock. She took the shaft in her mouth and began to suck gently. It stirred to life between her lips. He gasped and began to squirm beneath her. She pushed her sex toward his face, hoping he'd take advantage. He did, gripping her ass and pulling her pussy tightly to his mouth as he began to lick and suck her clit.

His cock grew in her mouth to full capacity as she sucked it. She drew her teeth along the shaft, nibbling at the tip. She teased the length of him before fisting her hands around the base and balls. With a moan, she began to suck harder, pulling at him as if he were a stubborn straw refusing to give her the drink she wanted.

Tension built in her stomach. Suddenly, he exploded between her lips. Lyra drank his essence as she came against his mouth.

"Wow," he whispered as she collapsed next to

him. She lightly nipped at his leg next to her head. His hand wrapped around her calf, holding her leg close to his chest. "I enjoyed that very much."

"I know," she chuckled, closing her eyes. Her body was relaxed and she did not fight the haze of sleep that came for her. And, as the final remnants of wakefulness left her, she heard his thought whispering in her head, *I love you, Lyra, only you, forever...*

CHAPTER 21
EPILOGUE

TWO YEARS LATER...

Lyra's hands trembled as she looked at the airtight metal chest. It had been sunk into the water exactly where she had specified in her letter to her family. Over a year had passed since she'd thrown the bottle onto shore, hoping one of her brothers would find it. She had almost not dared to hope that this day would come.

"Would you like me to open it for you?" Rigel asked. He sat down next to her on the couch in their palace apartment.

Lyra's hands shook too badly and she nodded.

Rigel leaned over and began to unlatch the sides. He'd hauled it in from his last hunt, carrying it directly to her. In fact, he was so fresh from the ocean

MICHELLE M. PILLOW

his hair was still wet and he smelled of salt. It took some doing, but finally the seal gave on the lid and he was able to lift the heavy piece of metal. Poking a finger inside the chest, he hooked a rolled paper and pulled out a letter. Without trying to read it, he handed it to her.

Lyra glanced into the chest. Thick plastic wrapped several everyday surface items. She slowly unrolled the message and let out a deep breath. "It's from Jackson. He's alive."

Rigel leaned into her, lifting his arm behind her back. She naturally cuddled against his side.

As she scanned the letter for news of her family, she said, "A ship picked him up three days after the wreck. He was afloat with Kristopher on a piece of driftwood. Rocky and Winston were rescued about a week later. Rocky spent a year in the hospital because of some injuries and Winston lost part of his leg, but they're both still alive. My father has retired from the sea. He lives on a beach in the Northwest United States. After sun exposure on the waves, he's had some trouble due to the severe dehydration, but he never complains." Lyra glanced up from the letter. "I can't believe they all made it. I hoped that one of them...but all?"

"This is very good news. The hunters will celebrate the good fortune." Suddenly, Rigel's smile fell. "Do you wish I would have left you at the surface with the others? You would have been rescued with your family. You would be on the surface world."

Lyra lowered the letter. "I do miss my family, and I can't tell you how much it means to me to hear that they are all right, but I can never regret my coming down to be with you, Rigel. I love you. That hasn't changed. You are as much a part of me as my own soul. We are fated. I don't know if it was the gods, or some mystical force, or even a miraculous accident that brought me down here to you, but I know that it is as it should be. You are my heart, Rigel. Never forget it."

"And you are mine," he said.

"Besides, Bridget has been busy working on analyzing that seaweed she found. She thinks she is close to discovering how the Olympians rise to the surface and breathe the air. Perhaps someday, I will see them again." She lightly touched her leg. "They will not believe my fins."

"I wonder if the surface world would welcome us," he mused, looking up.

Lyra didn't have the heart to tell him what the surface world would most likely do to a merman if they caught one.

"So it would be that bad for my kind, would it?" he asked.

"Stay out of my thoughts, husband. We've had this talk."

"And yet, I seem to recall seeing naked images of my wife sent to me while I was swimming back." He chuckled.

Lyra reached inside the chest and pulled out one of the packages. They were magazines. She handed them to Rigel. "Aidan will enjoy these."

Rigel slid them aside, moving to put his hands on her waist. "I'm afflicted. Now that we know your family is safe, can we first attend to—"

"Ah! He sent me a vacuum sealed pack of hotdogs!" Lyra exclaimed, teasing. She pulled out the food and grinned.

Rigel grabbed them and dropped them in the chest with a frown. "My woman has no need of—"

"It's a food," she laughed. Then, reaching to cup his hard shaft, she added, "I have all the man I need right here."

"Good." Rigel stood, lifting her in his arms as he carried her toward the shower. "Now I believe you promised to bathe me."

"I did no such thing." She didn't fight his embrace.

"I recall the details very vividly. One moment I am seeing a squid, the next my lovely wife is in my head imagining soaping me up."

"Oh, that promise," she moaned, as he sent her a delightfully wicked image. "I suppose there is time for your affliction." She nuzzled his throat and turned serious. "I'm very happy you are home. I missed you."

"As I you, Lyra. I carried you in my heart the entire trip."

She kissed his neck, sighing in happiness. "And I carry you in mine always."

The End

THE SERIES CONTINUES...

The Mighty Hunter
Commanding the Tides
Captive of the Deep
Surrender to the Sea
Making Waves
The Merman King

Surrender to the Sea
Lords of the Abyss Book 4

Atlantes, a lost city of intrigue to most, is Brutus's home, his curse, his prison. Doomed to an immortal life deep in the ocean, their only chance at salvation is to rescue damsels in distress from the surface world and bring them into the abyss. While mythology may label him and his kind monsters, this warrior is simply a man with needs. And he's found the perfect woman to see to them.

Chapter One Excerpt

As he watched yet another human flail beneath the ocean's surface, Brutus the Warrior wondered if killing them wouldn't be a kinder gesture than trying to push as many as he could to the top. All he could do was help them toward air and try to give them something solid to hold on to. The odds of being found by the surface world after a shipwreck were not in the mortals' favor. He felt no vibrations in the surrounding water that would indicate another vessel was near.

Humans were no match for his larger size. With his agility in the water, he would be able to swim up and snap their necks before they realized what had happened, or he could cut them with the razor sharp fin growing from his forearms. Every time he was forced to see this play of human death, he told himself to be kind, to kill them, to prevent suffering. And yet every time, he could not bring himself to do it. As fierce and big and monstrous as he would appear to these humans, he was none of those things. He was not a monster.

The scylla were the real monsters of the ocean—mindless souls lost in the sea, Merr people who had left home only to be cursed to search for something they'd never find. They were shadows in the water, almost impossible to perceive, harder to catch. Brutus was one of the few Merr hunters sent up to the ocean's surface to capture them. His brother Nemus had suffered the scylla fate for hundreds of years. It was why Brutus started hunting. They had trapped Nemus and had given his lost soul peace. As a hunter, it was Brutus's duty to save the humans, as if doing so enough times could somehow atone for his people's past.

He'd been hunting the creatures for a very long time, joined by his twin brother, Demon, and their younger brother, Rigel. Their team was called *Warriors*, and they made up one of the four units of hunters who were allowed to stray so close to the surface world. The hunting teams took turns every few weeks. Fourteen days was about the maximum time the mermen could stay in the open ocean without losing their minds.

The vibration of boats on open water drew the scylla. In the old days, the slide of the wooden hull and the rhythmic dip of oars had been like a dinner bell. With the right oceanic conditions and following the beat of oars, the Merr could track the young scylla easily. Back then, there were fewer crafts on the water—or maybe it just seemed that way. Now the subtle vibration of engines combined with the great distances ships could travel made hunting much more difficult. That, and the scylla were much older now.

They were all much older now.

Brutus wondered if his eternity would ever end, this infinite punishment of watching helplessly as person after person died. Yet, how could he stop doing his duty? Out of the tens upon tens of thousands he'd pushed to the surface, surely more than a few had survived.

When his sister-by-marriage's ship had gone down, he'd helped save her father and five brothers. Of course, they'd only found out the men had been rescued after Lyra had been brought down to Atlantes and condemned to their immortality. She couldn't return to her birth family, but had managed to make contact with her brothers on the surface world, something that had never been done in the history of Atlantes's curse. The confirmation that he'd been successful at least six times kept him going.

The white bottom of the small vessel finally gave way, creaking a last warning before sinking past him into the deep abyss below. At least, the screaming had stopped. He hated the screaming the most, the sound of their fear.

Brutus looked for his brothers in the water. Strips of sunlight filtered through from above, casting an eerie backdrop to kicking feet over his head.

Seeing the flash of black and silver of Demon's long tail, he dashed to follow. While Brutus saved the humans, Demon was tracking the scylla and Rigel would be nearby waiting to blow the vial of special liquid that would paralyze the creature so it could be brought back to Atlantes.

'It's fast,' Demon grumbled using the telepathic mind link.

'And strong,' Rigel warned. *'Be careful. It's pushed me twice.'*

'Circle it in,' Demon ordered. *'Brutus?'*

Brutus saw the glide of a shadow in the water and automatically darted in front of it to block the scylla's movement. Instead of rerouting, the creature slammed against Brutus like an ocean current, pushing him back with such force the merman couldn't stop his body as he was thrust up to the surface.

'*Stop it!*' Brutus yelled, knowing if he touched the surface air it could kill him. It would burn his flesh and if he inhaled it would scorch his lungs. It was the most effective way to kill his kind. The scylla was small but strong, and it propelled him upward, higher, higher. He struck his fist at it, but his hand slid through the shadow like water, and the creature did not stop.

'*Brutus!*' his brothers yelled in unison.

He saw the light from above. There was nothing he could do. This was it. '*It's been a good run, brothers. Bag this one and get his ass home.*'

'*Brutus, no!*'

To find out more about Michelle's books visit www.MichellePillow.com

ABOUT MICHELLE M. PILLOW

New York Times & *USA TODAY*
Bestselling Author

Michelle loves to travel and try new things, whether it's a paranormal investigation of an old Vaudeville Theatre or climbing Mayan temples in Belize. She believes life is an adventure fueled by copious amounts of coffee.

Newly relocated to the American South, Michelle is involved in various film and documentary projects with her talented director husband. She is mom to a fantastic artist. And she's managed by a dog and cat who make sure she's meeting her deadlines.

For the most part she can be found wearing pajama pants and working in her office. There may or may not be dancing. It's all part of the creative process.

Come say hello! Michelle loves talking with readers on social media!

www.MichellePillow.com

facebook.com/AuthorMichellePillow

twitter.com/michellepillow

instagram.com/michellempillow

bookbub.com/authors/michelle-m-pillow

goodreads.com/Michelle_Pillow

amazon.com/author/michellepillow

youtube.com/michellepillow

pinterest.com/michellepillow

COMPLIMENTARY EXCERPTS

CALL OF THE SEA EXCERPT
BY MICHELLE M. PILLOW

Call of the Lycan Series

Ian O'Connell, heir prince to his clan, has no plans to settle down even though his untamed nature keeps him on the prowl for female company. The only woman he could ever want saved him from a watery grave before disappearing from his life forever. But that was a long time ago, too long for a mortal woman to have survived. Though he searched for her, in the end it was in vain.

Cursed by the power of the Cancerian crab, Ceana is doomed to spend her eternity in the ocean as a mermaid. Her only relief is on a full moon, when she becomes human and must find shore. Centuries have passed and she's all but given up on the one who could save her. Brief passion is all she has and she's willing to take what she can get—especially if it's with an intriguing lycan who's untamed nature just might be her salvation.

Excerpt

Ian turned to his brother, James, barely catching his words. He grinned, knowing the guys were giving him a hard time for staring like the beast he was. In truth, any one of them would take Meghan to their bed but Ian knew they didn't. She refused them, choosing to save herself for him. He knew she wanted to be queen of the clans someday. Who knew, perhaps he would marry her. What else was he going to do? Pine for a woman whose face he couldn't recall?

Guilt assaulted him when he thought of her. The woman had saved his life. The least he could do was remember every detail of her pretty face. Ian closed his eyes, bringing forth her image the best he could. The exact details were a blur now, but he had the list in his mind. The moment had been brief, a flash in the middle of the night nearly a century ago. Long blonde waves almost silver by the light of the moon had surrounded him. Storm-weathered eyes, so round and large, shone in her perfect white skin. Her face was white as the snow, her lips red as blood.

Ian tried, but her face was still blurred by time. Her lips parted and she'd asked him something.

When were you born?

To this day, he didn't know what she had meant by that.

Laughter rose around him, and he opened his eyes.

James slapped him on the back, grinning. "Liquor too stout for you, brother?"

"Your jokes are too bad," Roark, the youngest of the three O'Connell brothers, said from their side. He looked like his older siblings, though was slightly shorter in stature and chose to wear his hair long to his waist, instead of short like Ian and James. Ian's own dark brown locks were chopped off at his shoulders and James' were cut even shorter than that— falling to just above his chin.

All of them had the broad shoulders and muscular bodies prevalent in their kind, especially the natural born. Humans who were changed were often slightly smaller because of their mortal heritage. The lycans took pride in themselves, in staying groomed and honoring their place in the lycan community, though they did have distinctly different styles. Ian preferred slacks and lightweight sweaters. James favored jeans and T-shirts and, much to his brothers' teasing, Roark wore leather—lots and lots of studded, black, biker-style leather.

They were an ancient people, their race as old as the human society, growing with the humans from a time when mortals knew of all the supernatural races. They used to be hunted, condemned as evil by the church. Sure, times were wilder in the early days, but so it was with all the races—mortal and supernatural. Just as humans no longer roamed the countryside pillaging and wielding swords, so did his people no longer wildly wield tooth and fang.

Now humans denied their existence, which suited most of them just fine. Occasionally, lines would be blurred and mortals would be turned. Lycans were lusty creatures after all, craving both blood and sex. Circumstances had to be right, the bloodline perfect, the moon full, for the bite to take effect. It was against the law to turn mortals. A lycan could attack fifty humans and only one would possibly start to turn, so if one was turned the odds were that lycan had attacked many before the changed one. Even then, it didn't guarantee they'd make it through the horrifically painful process. It's why his kind didn't mate with humans. Sure, they slept with them, dated them, some even spent lifetimes with them, but they didn't mate with them, not for all eternity. Only other immortal supernaturals were suitable lifemates. Too many lycans had seen their loved ones die as they tried to turn them. It was a painful memory that would be carried into eternity. For, if not murdered, the lycan would live forever.

Ian's brother helped to track down the rogue wolves who feasted on mortals, those who broke their laws—meager laws as they were. James was especially good at helping the newly turned to cope with their new gifts. He had a delicate way about him that the young ones responded to. Luckily, it had been many years since James' skill was called upon. The clan had been peaceful for the most part.

Thinking of feasting and sex, Ian looked at Meghan.

"I will gladly pursue her if she is too much lycan for you," Roark offered when Meghan pouted her lips at Ian for not coming to her as she beckoned him to do.

"Ah, you have no chance with that. She only parts her thighs for Ian. Her pussy is too refined for the likes of us," James grumbled. "You better watch yourself, brother, or you'll find yourself married to Meghan yet."

Ian raised a brow at his brother's distemper. It was no secret that James didn't like the woman. Sure, he'd fuck her if she offered—just like any of the males would—but he wouldn't like her as he was doing it.

"Relax," Ian said, laughing softly at James' suddenly foul mood.

"I'll relax when you cast her aside," James said. "That woman is too hungry for power—your power. I would not bow to her as my queen. Her heart is not pure and it definitely does not love you, just your future crown. I have no doubt that she would kill our father for the right to rule the clan."

"It's just sex, James," Ian assured him. It wasn't the first time he had done so. "Meghan knows that I do not love her as I have told her before."

"Then why bother?" Roark asked. "Take Brona or Dana. With the O'Connell charm I am sure they'd be most willing to bed you."

"Brona?" Ian shivered. "She's just now a century, merely a babe."

"And Dana's father is too protective of her,"

James said. "I would not have her father causing us trouble."

"Then how about Deirdre from the Macintyres? Or Padraigin MacConchobhair?" Roark offered, grinning in private thought.

"Padra?" James said. "Yes, she would make a fine choice."

Ian lifted a brow. "Play matchmaker with each other. I have an itch that I want Meghan to suck."

"I believe the word is scratch," Roark offered helpfully with a flip of his hair.

"Oh, she does that too." Ian winked, thrusting his mug over to James.

"But why her?" James protested.

Ian grinned. "Just look at her breasts."

Roark howled, James rolled his eyes and Ian made a move toward the sexy lycan in question. James didn't have to like Meghan. She was in Ian's bed, not his brother's. And the woman did enjoy sex —oral, anal, in any position he could bend her in. Why shouldn't he go to her?

When were you born?

Ian paused in mid-prowl. His head twitched to the side, listening past the fiddles and the flames, stretching out over the ocean waves. That voice. It was clearer now, not like before. It was as if he was hearing her for the first time.

Your name?

Ian tensed. He'd never caught her name, but part of him called out with his mind, hoping to give a name to the memory.

Who are you? Please. Answer me. Ask me again!

"Mmm, Your Royal Highness, why you gotta make a girl beg for it?"

Ian looked down as Meghan slid next to him. He hated when she called him "your royal highness" and such. It was only a reminder that she saw his title and his cock, not the man beneath both. But who was he to be picky when he was aroused and she was willing? Her nipples were already hard as they hit his chest. She rubbed her bikini-clad chest along his, until he could feel the buds though the thin material of his crimson sweater.

"Oh, Majesty, you seem to have an affliction. Come with me and let me tend to you." Flames glinted off her jet-black locks as she ran her hand down his chest to his stiff, protruding mass of flesh. Grasping his cock, her breathing deepened. Her eyes flashed completely golden. "You want to play tonight, don't you? I can feel the wolf starting to expand inside your pants. Come with me. Let me attend you, my prince. I will let you unleash the wolf tonight. I will let you take me as the beast."

Ian's nostrils flared. Meghan's feminine scent was strong and he knew her to be so wet that her bikini bottoms would be soaked with her cream. His body was willing, but his spirit was holding back. A feeling of mild disgust curled in him and he couldn't figure out why tonight, out of so many, he should find Meghan mildly repulsive.

Was it James' words? Was he tired of Meghan?

Tell me, when were you born?

No, it was her. He was sure he'd heard it that time. It couldn't be his imagination. Not again. She was human, he'd sensed it on her. But then how did she live so many years?

"Mmm," Meghan giggled, moving to wrap her arms around his neck. Ian grabbed her arms, stopping her. His eyes darted into the darkness, straining to see over the endless blue-black waves. The sun set completely, the edge of its golden purple light giving way to the blue of moonlit darkness. His body was tense, ready to run, to shift if he had to use more of his abilities.

The sea called to him and the moonlight shot into his skin, burning him. Sounds invaded him, becoming so loud he couldn't hear past the undulation of the waves, the faint sound of sand shifting over the beach with each powerful hit of the ocean. The sound of droplets spraying over the air became clear to him, like the tingling of ice in a glass. Ian tensed, waiting to hear it again, to hear her. The woman. His woman.

This can't be a dream.

"Ian?" Meghan gasped, confusion in her tone.

Ian pushed her back, irritated that she dared to enter his head with her voice. She stumbled and he instantly felt sorry, but he was too afraid to take his concentration off the distance.

"Ian!" Meghan demanded, her tone a hiss of breath as she growled at him in warning.

"You're not the one I want," he said, absently, not paying attention to the woman. The subtle sound of laughter rang all around him, distorted like a bad hallucination. In the distance he heard James and Roark above all others. He shut them out, again waiting for the water to give him its secrets.

Do you play tricks on me, ocean? Why do you call me to your depths? She cannot be there. She cannot.

A sensation washed over him. It was a strange feeling, but one he had known before. The urge was mindlessly beckoning him into the depths of the water. It had been the same that night he had almost died. The sea called him to her and he'd gone willingly into the murky waters only to be sucked in by the current. This time he held back. He was stronger now, could resist the call.

To find out more about Michelle's books visit www.MichellePillow.com

HIS FROST MAIDEN EXCERPT

BY MICHELLE M. PILLOW

Space Lords Book One
by Michelle M. Pillow

Bestselling Futuristic Romance Series

Empath and space pirate, Evan Cormier is obsessed with decoding an ominous premonition about his future. When a fellow crewman angered a spirit, the vengeful Zhang An took her wrath out on everyone in the vicinity. Evan just happened to be one of them. He's now facing a future in which he'll be forever alone.

Lady Josselyn of the House of Craven has been betrayed. With her home world on a Florencian moon under attack and her family dead, she finds herself at the mercy of the one who deceived them. There is only one thing left to do—die with honor. But before she can join her family in the afterlife, she must first avenge all that she held dear. Falling in love with a pirate was never in the plan. Evan and his thieving crewmates might have delayed her fate, but they can't stop destiny.

His Frost Maiden Excerpt

Craven Estates, Earth Settlement, Florencia's Fifth Moon

"Lift her," the General ordered, his shiny boots walking away from her, taking her reflection with it.

Two men hauled her to her feet, holding her up by her arms. Josselyn suppressed a cry as they jerked her dislocated shoulder. She couldn't see their faces, didn't need to. Her body hurt so badly she couldn't tell where the pain was coming from anymore.

The one who'd betrayed them stood before her. General Jack Stephans. He'd deceived her family and the fifth moon settlement. He'd traded them in for money and power. Josselyn lifted her gaze briefly to the hard depths of the steel green eyes before her. She wanted to kick, to give one last good blow, to go down fighting, but she couldn't raise her limbs.

"Poor little Josselyn, so heartbreaking," the General grabbed her chin and swiped beneath her eye. He looked young, was in fact very young for his position, only a few years older than her six and twenty. And yet they all knew so much more of fighting than anyone their age should, than anyone ever should.

"We gave you a home," she whispered. "How could you do this? How could you join them?"

"You gave me a place in your stables," he spat, his grip tightening on her chin, bruisingly so. "Not a place at your table. Not a place by your side. Not equal. They gave me a rank, a title. They give me respect. They give me a place in this world."

"Jack," she said, her voice softening for the orphan boy they'd found over twenty years ago. If she begged him, maybe fate could be turned around; maybe this day could be erased. Fate had spit them out in a whirlwind of chance and deceit. Maybe all that had happened wasn't his fault. Maybe it wasn't hers. None of it mattered. None of it changed the fact that he had taken everything she held dear, everyone, and now he was robbing her of her family home. Her tone hardened and she closed her eyes. "General."

"Look at me, Josselyn," he said. His tone caught even as his grip on her face tightened until his fingers pressed the inside of her cheeks against her teeth. "You're so cold. Even now, your face is composed. Is one, lonely tear all the passion you can muster?"

"I am Lady Josselyn of the House of Craven." Her eyes opened slowly, focusing on the shiny white of his uniform. It gleamed with the orange glow coming from the fireplace. The material looked odd in the drabber earth tones many on the fifth moon wore. Theirs was a world based on Medieval Earth. Each moon in the Florencian system was different, each settlement patterned off a singular time in the human past, times that history had almost forgotten. But the principals of the ancestors who'd established the colonies no longer applied. Times were different now. What had started as preservation of history had turned into reality, into laws and a way of life they all believed in as generation after generation was raised into the worlds of the Florencian moons.

The General shook her by the face until finally she forced her eyes to meet his. He looked angry, hurt, wildly hopeful. "I can save you. I can say you had nothing to do with the treachery of your family.

No one wants to kill a woman of noble blood. The line of Craven doesn't have to die. I will take your name; the name denied me by your father."

Was he serious? She knew he'd asked her father for her hand in marriage. In fact, she'd dismissed the proposal with the full knowledge he only asked because he wanted power. Did he think she could love him now? Want him? Take him into her bed?

He must have read the answer on her face because his own expression hardened. She knew Jack. He wouldn't ask again.

"I suppose not," he said, almost sad. "Even if you agreed, I could never trust you not to take a blade to my back. Not after today." He sighed heavily. "Not after this."

"Ago," she whispered, even her voice beginning to fail in its strength, "pugna quod int-"

"Quiet your tongue! This house is mine. Mine." He let go of her chin and her head drooped. "And you can die knowing that I have taken more than what you all refused to give me in life."

"A place at our table," Josselyn said, her tone softer still, the will to live leaving her. Her heart called out to her ancestors, to her dead family, begging them to come and get her.

"My table," he answered, stepping away. The

General lifted a gun, pointing it at her head. She heard the telltale click of metal on metal. The weapon was not one found on the fifth moon. They fought with swords and axes, like the old medieval ways. Though technology was available, not using it was a point of honor. He must have brought the weapon from another moon. Perhaps the Victorians? The Elizabethans? It appeared to be too old to be from much later in time.

"Do it, Jack." She didn't look at him as she waited for the final discharge of the gun, the loud bang before the end. When it didn't come, she repeated, the words a mere mouthing of her lips, "Do it."

"Speed you to a quick end, Josselyn Craven," Jack whispered. "You all brought this on yourselves."

To find out more about Michelle's books visit www.MichellePillow.com

REBELLIOUS PRINCE
BY MICHELLE M. PILLOW

Captured by a Dragon-Shifter Series

Catshifter Prince Rafe knows that technically he's supposed to be going to Earth to find a bride, but he doesn't see the need to rush things. While his dragon-shifter neighbors appear all too eager to claim their mates and settle down, he's all for putting that final moment off and enjoying his little trips through the portal. Yeah, yeah, eventually he'll have to marry and set a good example for his people because on his planet females are rare and they need to have children and blah blah blah. But honestly, catshifters are known to embrace their feral side and it would take a very impressive female to tame his.

Then he sees Jenna Kearney and all bets are off.

PLEASE LEAVE A REVIEW
THANK YOU FOR READING!

Please take a moment to share your thoughts by reviewing this book.

Be sure to check out Michelle's other titles at www.MichellePillow.com